THE CEM

by

Ivan Menchell

SAMUEL FRENCH, INC.
45 WEST 25TH STREET   NEW YORK 10010
7623 SUNSET BOULEVARD HOLLYWOOD 90046
LONDON   TORONTO

to the memory and laughter
that was my father, Lou

///

IMPORTANT BILLING AND CREDIT REQUIREMENTS

The Cemetery Club was originally produced as a work in progress by The Yale Repertory Theatre as part of Winterfest 7 on January 13, 1987. The production was directed by William Glenn, dramaturged by Jeff Magnin, and stage managed by Tom Aberger. The scenery was designed by Tamara Turchetta; costumes by Dunya Ramicova; lighting by Michael R. Chybowsky; sound by Ross S. Richards. The cast was as follows:

IDA.................................... Patricia Englund
LUCILLE............................... Sylvia Miles
DORIS .... Vera Lockwood
SAM..................................... Rod Colbin

The Cemetery Club was subsequently produced at The Cleveland Playhouse on May 16, 1989. The production was directed by Josephine R. Abady, dramaturged by Roger T. Danforth, and stage managed by Robert S. Garber. The scenery was designed by David Potts; costumes by Jane Greenwood and David Charles; lighting by Dennis Parichy; sound by Lia Vollack. The cast was as follows:

IDA.................................... Elizabeth Franz
LUCILLE............................ Nanette Fabray
DORIS .... Doris Belack
SAM............................... Eugene Troobnick
MILDRED........................... Joyce Krempel

The Cemetery Club was subsequently produced at The John F. Kennedy Center for the Performing Arts, Eisenhower Theatre on March 30, 1990. The production was presented by Howard Hurst, Philip Rose, Sophie Hurst and David Brown under the direction of Pamela Berlin and stage managed by Barbara-Mae Phillips. The scenery was designed by John Lee Beatty; costumes by Lindsay W. Davis; lighting by Natasha Katz; sound by Scott T. Anderson with music by Robert Dennis. The cast was as follows:

IDA...................................Elizabeth Franz
LUCILLE.............................Eileen Heckart
DORIS.................................Doris Belack
SAM....................................Lee Wallace
MILDRED............................Judith Granite

The production was then moved to the Brooks Atkinson Theatre in New York where it opened on May 12, 1990.

CHARACTERS

IDA
LUCILLE
DORIS
SAM
MILDRED

They are all in their late fifties to early sixties.

TIME

The time is mid-Autumn. The present.

PLACE

The action of the play takes place in the living room of Ida's house and at a cemetery in Forest Hills, Queens.

ACT I

Scene 1

SCENE: Ida's living room. The front door is USL leading to an open hallway running across the stage. USC is a staircase leading to the bedrooms. USR, at the opposite end of the hallway, is a chair and small desk on which is the telephone. On the upstage wall, bedside the door, is a hanging mirror and shelf. The living room is sunken DS of the hallway with a bay window SL looking out on to the street and an exit off right to the kitchen. There is also a curtained window in the wall USL that looks out on to the front porch and under which is the hi-fi. Separating the sunken living room from the hallway are some columns and a small bookshelf DS of the stairs. Just right of center is a couch with an end table, a chair and a coffee table. Left of the couch is an armchair with ottoman and a small humidor on which is a pipe rack and ash tray. In the bay window area is an upright piano and lamp. The piano is covered with framed photos of Ida's family. Downstage of the kitchen exit is a large side-board filled with knickknacks and dishes.

AT RISE: IDA comes down the stairs into the living room. The DOORBELL rings. As SHE goes to answer the door the OVEN TIMER rings offstage in the kitchen. SHE heads for the kitchen and the DOORBELL rings again. SHE's about to turn back for the door but decides that what's in the oven is more important. SHE exits to the kitchen. The DOORBELL rings again.

IDA. (*Offstage.*) Coming. Coming.

(*The DOORBELL rings again. IDA runs on holding her oven mitts.*)

IDA. I'm coming. (*Going for the door as the BELL rings again.*) I'm coming!

(*SHE opens the door. LUCILLE bursts in wearing a long fur coat.*)

LUCILLE. Son of a bitch!
IDA. What's the matter?!
LUCILLE. A guy follows me all the way from Queens Boulevard, undressing me with his eyes, and she asks what's the matter.
IDA. Again someone was following you?
LUCILLE. Can I help it if men find me attractive?
IDA. Who was it this time?
LUCILLE. I didn't get a name. He had blond hair, six one, six two, about a hundred seventy

pounds—a very nice build—with green eyes and a cleft chin—

IDA. What were you, walking backwards?

LUCILLE. I happen to have an excellent memory ... So what do you think?

IDA. I think you should just forget the whole thing.

LUCILLE. I mean about the *coat*. Look at this how she doesn't even notice.

IDA. Oh Lucille, it's beautiful. New?

LUCILLE. Have you seen it on this gorgeous body before?

IDA. You should wear it in the best of health.

LUCILLE. You ready for the best part? Guess how much.

IDA. A coat like that you must have paid at least three thousand.

LUCILLE. Nope.

IDA. Less?

LUCILLE. Much.

IDA. What, twenty-five hundred?

(*LUCILLE joyously shakes her head.*)

IDA. Don't tell me it was under two thousand.

LUCILLE. *Nineteen fifty*.

IDA. I'm fainting.

LUCILLE. Is that a steal or is that a steal?

IDA. Where did you find it?

LUCILLE. Well, I was walking in Manhattan down Fifty-seventh Street when I pass the Ritz Thrift Shop. Usually, I would never even look in the window. I mean, what could they have—garbage, right? This time I happen to look and what do you think I see?

IDA. That coat.

LUCILLE. No. I see a full length brown fox you could die from. I go in, try it on and my mazel it's a little too tigh— (*She's about to say "tight" but stops herself.*)—short. Then as I'm walking out, I'm looking down the rack and what do you think catches my eye?

IDA. That coat.

LUCILLE. A leopard jacket that made my heart stop. But for how often I'd get to wear it, it didn't pay.

IDA. Lucille, we're not getting any younger. Where did you find the mink?

LUCILLE. So, as I'm about to leave I see them bringing in a new rack and what do you think is the first thing I spot?

IDA. Who knows?

LUCILLE. This coat.

IDA. Thank God.

LUCILLE. There's only one thing that bothers me.

IDA. What?

LUCILLE. Knowing it was someone else's. I mean, who knows who this person is? All I know is that she's tall, terrifically slim and probably didn't look half as good in it as I do.

IDA. So what are you worried? You got a gorgeous coat at a great price.

LUCILLE. Ida, why would she give this coat up?

IDA. Who knows? Maybe she died.

LUCILLE. Oh my God. I didn't even think. This poor woman could be dead. For all I know, she could have died in this coat. The poor thing could've been wearing this coat, crossing the street and got hit by a car. It's not marked anywhere, is it? (*SHE turns around to show Ida the back of the coat.*)

IDA. It's perfect. Not a scratch on it ... except for that one tire mark down the back.

LUCILLE. Oh!

IDA. I'm only kidding. There's nothing on it. Let me try it on.

LUCILLE. My pleasure.

(*LUCILLE takes off the coat and gives it to Ida. SHE puts it on.*)

IDA. How do I look?

LUCILLE. Do the words "Lana Turner" mean anything?

IDA. Let me see.

(*SHE runs over to the mirror and looks at herself. LUCILLE stands behind her.*)

LUCILLE. What becomes a legend most!

IDA. (*Embarrassed.*) Oh ...

LUCILLE. Maybe I'll take a look, see if they have another one. Picture the two of us out on the town, fur from head to toe.

IDA. It's not me.

LUCILLE. All the more reason.

IDA. I don't need it. (*SHE takes off the coat and hangs it up.*)

LUCILLE. Ida, no one buys a mink because they need it. You buy support hose because you need it. You buy a mink because you *want* it.

IDA. I don't want it. Besides, I couldn't afford it. Where did *you* get two thousand dollars?

LUCILLE. One of Harry's Municipals Bonds came due.

IDA. Well, congratulations. How about some tea?

LUCILLE. Love it.

IDA. I'll put the water up.

(*SHE exits to the kitchen. LUCILLE hangs the coat in the closet.*)

LUCILLE. I want you to know I broke a pretty hot date to come here today.

IDA. (*Offstage.*) Who you got now?

LUCILLE. His name's Donald. Ida, if I tell you.

IDA. Good looking?

LUCILLE. *Gorgeous* ... (*Nonchalantly looking through Ida's mail.*) and a gentleman. Opens the door, pulls out the chair, picks up the check. We had a night Friday you wouldn't believe. Dinner, dancing, a hansom cab ride through Central Park.

IDA. (*Reenters*.) How romantic.

LUCILLE. And he didn't leave me alone all night. Hands everywhere.

IDA. No.

LUCILLE. Yeah.

IDA. So when do I meet him already?

LUCILLE. You'll meet him.

IDA. You never stay with one long enough for me to meet them.

LUCILLE. I'll tell you what – if we're still together next week I'll have him stop by during canasta. And what about you? When am I going to start hearing about a little romance, a little excitement?

IDA. When it happens you'll hear about it.

LUCILLE. I'm all ready to start double dating. I can't keep taking out two men by myself.

IDA. Why, they get tired?

(*THEY laugh.*)

LUCILLE. I'm serious, Ida. I'm waiting for you to join me. God knows Doris is never going to start.

IDA. I wonder where she is. It's after eleven. I figured she would've been here early. Today's an important day for her.

LUCILLE. It's always important to Doris. This is the high point of the month for her. She thinks about it for two weeks after and starts getting ready two weeks before. It's like a vicious cycle.

IDA. Sometimes a cycle is important. You know what to expect.

LUCILLE. Well, my cycle ended more years ago than I care to remember and that hasn't stopped me.

IDA. I just hope today goes well, I can't believe it's already her fourth anniversary.

LUCILLE. *Today's* her fourth anniversary? I completely forgot.

IDA. How could you?

LUCILLE. I can't keep up with the dates anymore.

IDA. You really should try.

LUCILLE. Sometimes I think we should stop this whole business altogether.

IDA. Lucille.

LUCILLE. I do.

IDA. ... I don't know myself anymore.

LUCILLE. You see.

IDA. So why do you keep coming?

LUCILLE. Don't think I haven't asked myself.

IDA. I'm serious.

LUCILLE. I like this time together.

(*IDA smiles.*)

LUCILLE. But I'm sure there's other ways we could spend the afternoon.

(*The DOORBELL rings.*)

IDA. (*Going to the door.*) Well don't bring it up today.

LUCILLE. I wouldn't say a word. Whatever she wants to talk, we'll talk.

IDA. You're a good friend.

LUCILLE. The best.

(*IDA opens the door. DORIS enters wearing a dark skirt suit and hat and carries a coat over her arm and a small folding stool.*)

IDA. Where have you been?

DORIS. Fine thank you and how are you?

(*THEY kiss hello.*)

LUCILLE. We've been worried sick here.

IDA. What took you so long?

DORIS. I overslept

IDA. *Today?*

(*DORIS and LUCILLE kiss.*)

DORIS. I didn't sleep too good last night. Did you get another bill for perpetual care?

IDA. You mean besides the one in the spring?

DORIS. Yeah.

IDA. No.

DORIS. (*To Lucille.*) How about you?

LUCILLE. I haven't paid the spring one yet. When Blue Cross pays *me* for Harry being sick I'll pay the *cemetery* for Harry being dead.

DORIS. Well, you'll probably get yours Monday. I'm not even going to tell you how high it's gone up.

IDA. Again it's gone up?

LUCILLE. And what are they going to do if we don't pay? What, they going to move them?

(*The tea KETTLE whistles.*)

DORIS. You want me to make?

IDA. Sit. I'll get it.

(*IDA exits to the kitchen. DORIS hangs up her coat then joins Lucille on the couch.*)

DORIS. So how are you?

LUCILLE. Good. You look different.

DORIS. I dropped a couple of pounds.

LUCILLE. You're losing weight?

DORIS. No, it's just moving lower. So what do you think of this day?

LUCILLE. Nice.

DORIS. Nice? A more beautiful day hasn't been invented. The leaves are just starting to fall. The colors are incredible. Abe's plot is going to look gorgeous. I just hope they kept up the care. You remember the argument I had with them last month. He's telling me they water twice a week while I'm looking down at dead ivy.

LUCILLE. I'm sure it'll look terrific.

DORIS. Funny, you know, fall was Abe's favorite time of year.... Eh, a wonderful man taken much too soon.

LUCILLE. Who could believe? *Four years ago today.*

DORIS. You remembered. I didn't think you'd remember.

LUCILLE. Of course I remembered. How could I forget? It was almost exactly a year before my Harry died.

DORIS. That's Murry.

LUCILLE. What's Murry?

DORIS. Murry. *Ida's* Murry. *He* died the year before your Harry.

LUCILLE. *Murry* died the year before Harry?

DORIS. Of course, Abe died two years before Murry.

LUCILLE. So Harry died three years after Abe.

DORIS. That's what I'm trying to tell you.

LUCILLE. So who died the year before Murry?

DORIS. No one.

LUCILLE. You sure?

DORIS. Of course I'm sure! Abe died four years ago today.

LUCILLE. That's what I said. Four years ago today. Who could forget? A wonderful man taken much too soon.

DORIS. They were all wonderful men. I wonder what the three of them are doing now?

LUCILLE. Probably looking for a fourth to play cards.

(*As THEY laugh, IDA enters with the tea and a plate of cookies on a tray.*)

IDA. So what are we talking? (*SHE sets the tray down on the coffee table and hands out the cups.*)

LUCILLE. We're trying to figure out what the boys are doing right now.

IDA. Murry is easy. Right now he's sitting, smoking a cigar and any minute his ash is going to fall and burn a small hole in a cloud.

LUCILLE. Let's see ... Today's Sunday, so Harry'll go right for the Manhattan real estate section then yell for half an hour how thirty years ago he could've bought a brownstone on Park Avenue for twenty-five thousand dollars.

DORIS. Abe is definitely out on a walk. Sunday was his day for walking, so wherever they walk up there, that's where he is.

IDA. Here's to the boys ... wherever they are.

(*THEY all raise their cups, toast, and drink.*)

DORIS. Funny, you know, I was reading last week how this woman contacts the dead through a ... a what do you call it? You hold hands in a circle around a big table. Like a seder.

LUCILLE. Seance.

DORIS. That's it. She says she actually talks to them. You have to put something that belonged to the deceased on the table, or a picture.

LUCILLE. I don't believe in that.

IDA. I don't know. I've heard some pretty interesting things.

DORIS. I think one day I'm going to try it. Wouldn't it be something if I could contact Abe, if I could talk with him? Even if just for a few minutes.

IDA. I don't know if I'd want to contact Murry.

DORIS. Why not?

LUCILLE. Because it unnatural. Your husband dies, that's it. The time for talking is finished.

DORIS. Unnatural is a man dying in his prime. You get married so you can spend the rest of your life with someone you love.

LUCILLE. You get married 'til "death do you part."

IDA. If I could contact Murry I'd like to ask him what he would've done, if I had gone first. I wonder if he would remarry.

DORIS. Abe, never.

IDA. I think Murry would. (*To Lucille.*) What about Harry, you think he would?

LUCILLE. I couldn't care less. The only thing I'd like to ask Harry is if maybe there's a bank account somewhere he forgot to tell me about. What difference does it make whether or not he'd remarry?

IDA. Oy, that reminds me. I completely forgot. I spoke to Selma this morning—

LUCILLE. No.

DORIS. Don't tell me.

IDA. She's getting married.

LUCILLE. I don't believe it.

DORIS. At her age.

IDA. Just goes to show you, you're never too old.

DORIS. *She's* too old.

IDA. She's the same age as I am.

DORIS. I rest my case.

IDA. Oh, you want to start talking age? After all, next month you're going to be—

DORIS. Don't you dare.

LUCILLE. It's like watching my two older sisters fight.

IDA. You keep out of this. You're only three days younger than dirt.

LUCILLE. Look who's talking. I was there when you celebrated your fiftieth birthday for the fourth time.

IDA. I did no such thing.

DORIS. Oh yes you did.

IDA. I am very proud of my age. I happen to think I look pretty terrific.

LUCILLE. You do. I hope *I* look as good as you do at your age.

IDA. You did.

DORIS. (*To Lucille.*) I just hope I *reach* your age.

LUCILLE. (*To Doris.*) You've been my age twice.

DORIS. (*To Lucille.*) And *you've* been your age since I know you.

IDA. Can we call it a tie on this one?

DORIS. Fine.

LUCILLE. It's all right by me.

IDA. Now where was I?

LUCILLE. Selma's getting married.

IDA. So I told her we would all be there.

LUCILLE. Of course.

DORIS. We've never missed one of Selma's weddings.

IDA. That's what I figured. She also asked if we could be bridesmaids.

DORIS. You're kidding.

LUCILLE. I don't know her *that* well.

DORIS. What happened to the women she used last time?

IDA. She doesn't like to use the same bridesmaids for more than one wedding. It's bad luck. Why don't the two of you come over here? We'll change and all go together.

LUCILLE. Why not?

DORIS. Sure.

LUCILLE. When's the affair?

IDA. Month after next.

DORIS. So soon? She only met Arnold over the summer.

IDA. She's not marrying Arnold. She's marrying Ed.

DORIS and LUCILLE. Who's Ed?

IDA. Some man she met a couple of weeks ago on a singles weekend. She says they're madly in love. And are you ready for this? His name is Ed *Bonfigliano*.

DORIS and LUCILLE. Bonfigliano?

DORIS. That's not a Jewish name.

IDA. He's not a Jewish man.

DORIS. Selma *Bonfigliano* ...? What happened to Arnold?

IDA. He died.

LUCILLE. So Selma's marrying an Italian.

DORIS. Go figure.

IDA. Well, she never did like being alone. Selma always said she felt lonely being by herself in that house.

DORIS. If you don't like to be alone you get a dog not an Italian.

IDA. I don't know. Maybe she has the right idea.

LUCILLE. What are you talking? The woman goes through husbands like I go through nylons.

IDA. Look who's talking.

LUCILLE. Dating is one thing. Marriage is something else.

DORIS. I have to agree there.

LUCILLE. So when are you going to start?

DORIS. Don't push it. I think it's time we should be going. I don't want to be late.

LUCILLE. What, if you're a little late he leaves?

(*DORIS gives her a look.*)

LUCILLE. I'm sorry.

IDA. (*Puts the cups back on the tray and heads off to the kitchen. Offstage.*) It's cold out?

LUCILLE. A little chilly.

DORIS. It's perfect. The cemetery'll look gorgeous and if Abe's ivy is dead, heads are going to roll.

IDA. (*Reentering.*) It'll be fine, I'm sure.

(*THEY get their coats out of the closet, and put them on.*)

LUCILLE. (*Showing off her coat.*) So Doris, what do you think of the coat?

DORIS. Gorgeous.

LUCILLE. Guess how much.

DORIS. For something like that, if it's second-hand and you got a good price, with a little haggling you should've paid maybe, what, nineteen hundred?

(*LUCILLE, annoyed, opens the door and exits in a huff. DORIS smiles at Ida as SHE picks up her folding stool. THEY exit with IDA closing the door behind them as the LIGHTS fade out.*)

Scene 2

*The cemetery. The graves are lined up across the
stage so that the rows of headstones are parallel
to the audience. Abe's grave (Doris' husband)
is DSL and faces upstage. Murry's grave Ida's
husband) is DSR and faces downstage.
Harry's grave (Lucille's husband) is US right
of center and faces upstage. On all headstones,
where the front are visible, the names should
be Jewish with Jewish symbols and Hebrew
writing if possible. There are two engraved
stone blocks DSC marking a path way running
upstage. DSL, between the block and Abe's
grave, is a stone bench. There are many shrubs
and bushes of ivy between the graves and at
least one tree (lots of colored leaves for Act I
and bare for Act II.) Behind the cemetery,
which should appear to extend far beyond the
area the women are in, we see a highway and
the remnants from the World's Fair at Flushing
Meadow park (the unisphere and sky
restaurants). Further in the distance we can see
the Manhattan skyline. (NOTE: Because the
cemetery is in Queens near LaGuardia Airport,
the audience should hear the sound of planes
flying overhead.)*

*The day is just as Doris described it. It is not too
cold yet and the leaves have just started turning
to their brilliant colors.*

*DORIS, IDA and LUCILLE enter. DORIS carries
her small folding stool.*

LUCILLE. How could you not notice that gorgeous man standing by the mausoleum?

IDA. I didn't notice.

LUCILLE. I'm telling you, he didn't take his eyes off me.

DORIS. (*Taking it all in.*) What a day. Beautiful, just beautiful. Why don't the two of you meet me at Abe's plot when you're finished. We'll have a little gathering for the fourth anniversary.

IDA. We'd love to.

LUCILLE. Of course.

DORIS. See you later. (*Walks to Abe's grave.*)

IDA. (*To Lucille.*) I think she's handling it very well.

LUCILLE. A lot better than last year.

IDA. You remember how we had to carry her out?

LUCILLE. Who could forget? One minute she was doing fine, the next she's laying belly up on her plot next to Abe's screaming, "Take me now!"

IDA. I think she's over that.

LUCILLE. I hope so.

IDA. I'm going over to Murry.

LUCILLE. Give him my best.

(*THEY walk off in different directions. By this point the LIGHTS have come up on DORIS who is sitting on her stool, picking leaves out from the ivy that covers Abe's grave.*

NOTE: Although the graves will have to be close together on stage, it should be made clear that the women can neither hear nor see one another.)

DORIS. Perpetual care, my foot. Perpetual negligence is what it is! Look at this how I can't even see the dates. If I didn't come every month you'd be laying here underneath a jungle. (*SHE takes out a pair of scissors from her handbag and begins trimming the ivy.*) Whenever I cut the ivy like this I think of how I used to trim your hair in the kitchen. Remember ...? A little off the back. A little off the sides. Don't go near the front or make the part too wide.

(*LIGHTS up on Ida at Murry's grave.*)

IDA. Doris was right. It looks beautiful. We couldn't have picked a nicer spot. Funny, when I'm here with you, knowing Doris is with Abe and Lucille's with Harry, it feels like we're all together again—like old times. Reminds me of the cruises the six of us used to take. You, Harry, and Abe would gamble while we shopped from one end of St. Thomas to the other.

(*LIGHTS up on Lucille at Harry's grave as SHE lights up a cigarette.*)

LUCILLE. So Harry, read any good books lately ...? I suppose I'll have to do all the talking again. Nice. Like when we were married. Except now at least I know where you are every night.

(*DORIS finishes cutting and puts the scissors back in her bag.*)

IDA. Murry, sometimes it worries me, the memories being that strong. It makes it so hard to—I don't know.

DORIS. So let's see, what happened since we spoke last? Oh, Selma's getting married again.

LUCILLE. I just want you to know Harry, things could have changed. All we needed was time. But everything you had to do in a hurry. You couldn't even go into remission like a normal person. No, you had to get it all over with— *Quick.*

IDA. I look at Lucille and wonder if maybe she doesn't have the right idea. I'm not saying I want to start having flings. Lucille I'm not. I just don't think it's right to close myself off anymore.

LUCILLE. (*Sadly.*) Just a little time and everything would've straightened itself out.

DORIS. Oh, you'll never guess who's chasing the women. You ready for this? Max. Max Goldberg! At seventy-six he's decided to take up chasing the girls. So I asked his wife what she's going to do about it and you know what she told me? She said, "He's seventy-six. Who cares if he's chasing women? Dogs chase cars but when they catch them they can't drive."

IDA. The thing is, Murry, I don't know if I could start going out, meeting people, and ... and also keep coming to see you.

LUCILLE. So Harry, what do you think of the coat you just bought me? Am I a knockout or what?

DORIS. Oh, I almost forgot. I got a new picture.

(As DORIS gets a small photograph out from her purse A MAN, in his mid-sixties, passes by Lucille.)

LUCILLE. Hello there.
MAN. Hello.
LUCILLE. Come here often?

(No reaction.)

LUCILLE. Just a little cemetery humor.
DORIS. *(Showing the photo to Abe.)* Just look at your grandson.
LUCILLE. So, your wife, she stays at home while you go to the cemetery?
MAN. My wife is who I come to visit.
LUCILLE. Oh, how nice.
MAN. I really should get going.
LUCILLE. I was just leaving. Come, we'll walk together.

(THEY exit.)

IDA. I wonder what you're doing while I'm standing here talking. If you're up there listening, smoking a cigar.

DORIS. Sometimes I see David playing with a toy in the living room. With such concentration he sits.

IDA. How I used to yell at you for smoking in the bedroom. To this day I can still smell it every once in a while.

DORIS. He looks just like you did when you'd try, for hours, to fix some gadget. I can still picture you at your desk.

IDA. It's been over two years.

DORIS. Four years.

IDA. And sometimes it seems like—

DORIS. (*Smiling.*) You're still right there.

IDA. (*Sadly.*) You're still right there. (*Pause.*) If next month I don't come, Murry—I'm not saying I won't but if ... *if* I shouldn't be here, promise me you wouldn't be upset

DORIS. You know, one day I think I'll bring David.

IDA. You were a wonderful man, Murry—

DORIS. —To talk to his grandfather.

IDA. —Another one like you I wouldn't find.

(*DORIS puts the photo away. LUCILLE enters near Murry's grave with the MAN.*)

LUCILLE. So help me, nineteen fifty and *no tax*.

MAN. It's a very nice coat.

LUCILLE. Come here. I want you to meet—

MAN. Ida?

IDA. Sam.

LUCILLE. You two know each other?

IDA. Of course. This is Sam. The best butcher in the whole world. How are you?

SAM. Good. And you?

IDA. Fine. You came to see Merna?

SAM. Yeah.

IDA. Doris is over at Abe's. It's the fourth anniversary today.

DORIS. *Four years.*

SAM. You think it would be all right if I went over?

IDA. I think she'd love it.

LUCILLE. Come, I'll walk you.

(*SHE takes his arm as the THREE of them begin walking toward Doris.*)

IDA. Oy, wait. I forgot. (*Runs back to the grave and picks up a small stone.*)

DORIS. How did I get his far?

IDA. I'll uh ... I'll see you when I see you.

(*SHE kisses the stone then places it on Murry's headstone then rejoins LUCILLE and SAM as THEY walk over to Doris.*)

DORIS. Abe, I got a pain here that hasn't gone away in four years. So many things I miss.

(*SHE bends down as LUCILLE, IDA and SAM approach.*)

LUCILLE. (*Running over.*) Quick! She's going to lie down again!

IDA. (*Running over.*) Doris, don't do it! Don't lie down!

DORIS. Do what?! Who's lying?! I was *bending* to pick up a stone. You scared me half to death. Hello, Sam.

SAM. Hello Doris.

DORIS. It's good to see you.

SAM. I wanted to pay my respects.

DORIS. Today is four years, you know.

SAM. Ida told me.

DORIS. I'd like to just stand in silence for a few minutes to think, remember, and hopefully get my heart rate back down.

IDA. We're right here with you, Doris.

DORIS. It's nice to have such good friends.

LUCILLE. You've got the best.

SAM. Maybe I should go.

DORIS. Don't be silly. Abe would be honored.

LUCILLE. You're not going anywhere.

(*SHE pulls him over and puts her arm through his as THEY all stand in silence and look down at Abe's grave. After a long moment LUCILLE begins talking to Sam in a loud whisper.*)

LUCILLE. So what are you doing later?

SAM. (*Politely.*) Shhh.

LUCILLE. (*Pause.*) Why don't you join us for a little—

IDA. Lucille.

LUCILLE. (*Pause.*) Better yet, maybe you and I could—

DORIS. I don't believe you.

LUCILLE. I'm just trying to make Sam feel comfortable.

DORIS. Stop flirting, he'll feel comfortable.

IDA. Lucille, really.

LUCILLE. Well how much longer are we—

DORIS. I'm sorry to inconvenience you. I would just like to have a few minutes of silence for my husband who died four years ago today.

SAM. Maybe I should go.

IDA. It's not you, Sam.

LUCILLE. Stay where you are.

DORIS. Look, you want to pick up men, do it at another grave!

IDA. *Doris.*

SAM. I don't want to cause any—

LUCILLE. What am I standing here for? What, just because Abe kicked off four years ago today I have to take this kind of abuse?! (*Shouting to Abe's grave.*) Happy anniversary! (*SHE storms off.*)

IDA. Lucille!

SAM. I really—

DORIS. The whole day is ruined—

IDA. Doris—

DORIS. (*Grabbing her stool.*) —Shot to hell!

SAM. I think I left something—

DORIS. (*Yelling to Lucille as SHE exits.*) I hope your coat falls apart!!

IDA. Doris! (*SHE runs after them and exits, leaving Sam standing alone at Abe's grave.*)

SAM. (*To Abe's grave.*) And you thought you were going to rest in peace. (*HE exits as the LIGHTS fade out.*)

Scene 3

Ida's house. Late afternoon.
The door opens and IDA rushes in carrying three handbags. Leaving the door open, SHE runs into the living room and hides two of the bags under the couch. SHE returns to the door and yells outside as SHE takes off her coat.

IDA. You're not getting your bags back until you both come in here!

(*SHE hangs up her coat then goes to the couch, sits down, and picks up a magazine. LUCILLE enters angrily and walks over to a chair and sits. DORIS enters shortly after, closes the door and remains standing, holding on to her stool. There is a moment of silence as IDA thumbs through the magazine.*)

IDA. (*Without looking up.*) It says here that if two women who have been good friends for over twenty years don't make up immediately, a third friend is going to kill them both.

DORIS. If you read carefully it also says that one of the two women, the promiscuous one, did something unforgivable at the other woman's husband's grave.

LUCILLE. If you look at the title of the story it's called "Doris lives with her head in the ground where all she sees is *Abe*."

DORIS. I would like my handbag back now please.

IDA. No one is getting a thing until this business is straightened out.

DORIS. Everything is straightened out. I'm never speaking to her again so there won't be any problems.

IDA. (*To Lucille.*) Why don't you just apologize?

LUCILLE. Why should I apologize? For meeting a charming man with whom I had a wonderful rapport?

DORIS. Maybe she would like for me to turn Abe's plot into a singles' bar.

IDA. What do you mean, a wonderful rapport?

LUCILLE. You should have seen the way he couldn't take his eyes off me at Harry's grave.

IDA. You're kidding.

LUCILLE. No.

DORIS. Ida, I think you're missing the issue here. I was trying to have a moment of silence for my husband who happened to die four years ago today.

LUCILLE. For Chrissakes Doris, you stand at Abe's grave like he died yesterday.

DORIS. And that is the way I will stand every month.

LUCILLE. Good, so from now on you can do it without me. As of today I officially resign from this ... this ... *cemetery* club!

IDA. Lucille.

LUCILLE. (*Taking off her coat.*) I mean it. I've had it to here with the goddamn cemetery! I refuse to be in a club in which half the members are dead!

DORIS. That's a terrible thing to say.

LUCILLE. Because it's the truth.

DORIS. No it's not!

LUCILLE. What do you mean it's not? I can guarantee if you took a roll call right now, three of the members would be marked absent.

DORIS. And that is why we go visit them every month.

LUCILLE. Well, instead of visiting the old members we should be out there scouting for new applicants.

DORIS. I don't believe what I'm hearing! Ida, will you talk some sense into this woman?!

(*IDA doesn't answer.*)

DORIS. Ida.

(*No answer.*)

DORIS. *Ida*.

IDA. (*Pause*.) Maybe ... maybe it is time we stopped.

DORIS. What are you talking?

IDA. For a while. Maybe ... maybe we need a break.

DORIS. Ida, do you realize what you just said? (*To Lucille*.) It's your fault. This is all your fault! (*To Ida*.) This woman is like poison to you. (*To Lucille*.) *You* told her to stop going to the cemetery!

LUCILLE. I did no such thing.

DORIS. Don't tell me!

IDA. Lucille never said a word. Doris, look at us. It's been over two years since Murry died, four years since Abe and what do we have to show for it? We've seen every movie that's come out, become experts at canasta, and I know Murry's headstone like the back of my hand. Do you realize how much time we've spent at the cemetery?

LUCILLE. Let me ask you something, Doris. Don't you ever feel like you sometimes miss having a man around?

DORIS. *You* I'm not listening to.

IDA. But Doris, don't you ever feel like you'd like to have someone there, someone new,—

LUCILLE. Someone *living*.

DORIS. Abe and I gave each other our lives, Ida.

IDA. I know—

DORIS. Our *lives*. I have nothing to give to another man. Everything I gave to Abe and still give. And *once a month* I let him know.

IDA. But getting married again wouldn't mean you loved Abe any less. You wouldn't marry someone now for the same reasons you married Abe.

DORIS. I wouldn't marry someone now period. The case is closed.

LUCILLE. (*To Ida.*) What are you in such a hurry to get married? The thing to do now is to get out there again and ... and play the field.

IDA. What field?

LUCILLE. It's an expression. It means you should be dating, going out with different men.

DORIS. It's a stupid expression and a stupid idea.

IDA. Dating?

DORIS. Can you believe her?

IDA. I wouldn't even know what to do.

LUCILLE. It's like riding a bicycle.

DORIS. This whole conversation is ridiculous.

LUCILLE. To *you*.

DORIS. (*Hanging up her coat.*) All of a sudden Sam, the playboy butcher, shows up at the cemetery and the two of you go crazy.

IDA. Doris—

DORIS. I would expect it from this one. (*Indicating Lucille.*) but you ... you, I'm shocked.

IDA. Doris, there's nothing to be shocked about. No one's going crazy. We're just talking. And I would hardly call Sam a playboy.

DORIS. No? then what was he doing at the cemetery?

IDA. What do you mean what was he doing at the cemetery? He was visiting Merna.

DORIS. Hah! He hasn't been to her grave in over a year. The only reason he goes to the cemetery is to try to meet a woman.

IDA. Don't be ridiculous.

DORIS. Ridiculous? You don't remember Rose Jacobs?

IDA. I remember Rose Jacobs. I don't remember them meeting at the cemetery.

DORIS. Less than five feet away from Mel's grave.

LUCILLE. I like his style.

DORIS. And how about Sylvia Green? Where do you think they met?

LUCILLE. He went out with Sylvia Green?

DORIS. (*To Ida.*) Am I lying?

(*IDA doesn't answer.*)

DORIS. And it all started at the unveiling of Lou's headstone. He caught her in the middle of mourning and went out with her later that night.

IDA. I'm sure it didn't happen that fast.

DORIS. So maybe my timing's a little off but the place I remember. He got her at the cemetery.

*(The BELL rings. IDA opens the door and SAM
enters carrying a brown paper bag.)*

IDA. Sam.

SAM. Ida.

LUCILLE. Hi, Sam.

SAM. *(Not expecting her.)* Oh, hello Lonnie.

LUCILLE. *Lucille.*

SAM. Lucille. I'm sorry. I've got no memory
for names. *(Spotting Doris.)* Hello Doris.

DORIS. *(Knowingly, slightly disdainful.)*
Hello, Sam.

SAM. I uh ... I didn't realize you would all be
here. Maybe I should come back some other time.

IDA. No, please come in.

SAM. *(Awkwardly.)* I uh ... I remembered the
chicken livers you wanted so I put some aside on
Friday and I figured since I'm in the
neighborhood I'd ... I'd drop them off.

IDA. That was very nice.

SAM. Maybe I should just leave it and go.

IDA. Don't be silly. *(Closing the door and
taking the bag.)* I was just going to put some tea
on. You'll have a cup. *(SHE exits to the kitchen.)*

LUCILLE. *(Taking off his coat and hanging it
in the closet.)* So, a butcher that delivers. What
more could a girl want?

SAM. *(To Doris.)* I'm sorry about what
happened at the cemetery. I shouldn't have been
there.

LUCILLE. Don't be silly. It was nice having a new face. Come, sit. (*Escorts Sam to the couch and sits beside him.*)

SAM. I feel like I ruined a very special moment for the three of you.

LUCILLE. What special? We go every month.

SAM. Every month?

LUCILLE. I understand that you also enjoy going to the cemetery.

SAM. Sometimes I feel a need.

DORIS. I'm sure you do.

IDA. (*Enters carrying a plate of cookies.*) So what are we talking?

LUCILLE. Sam and I were just discussing how sometimes one feels a need to go to the cemetery.

IDA. (*Surprised.*) I see.

LUCILLE. (*Suddenly.*) I think I have a terrific idea.

IDA. What's that?

LUCILLE. Well, since Sam here goes to the same cemetery to visit his lovely wife, uh ...

SAM. Merna.

LUCILLE. Merna. Why don't the four of us go together next month?

SAM. I—

IDA. I thought we decided not to go.

SAM. I—

DORIS. It's supposed to be the three of us.

SAM. I—

LUCILLE. (*To Doris.*) Who put you in charge of the rule book?

SAM. Look, I really don't know when I'll want to go again. But I'm flattered you should ask.

IDA. Actually, we might not even be going next month.

DORIS. *You* might not be going.

IDA. We were just discussing the fact that it might be time to stop.

LUCILLE. We were saying that there comes a time you have to leave the cemetery and play the field.

SAM. What field?

DORIS. (*To Sam.*) Thank you.

LUCILLE. I mean, there comes a time you have to stop going to the cemetery and start dating again. Before you came we were having a little discussion about it. What are your feelings?

(*All three WOMEN turn to Sam. The weight of his response is apparent.*)

SAM. (*Nervously. Diplomatically.*) I uh ... I think that ... that you have to do what's right for you. (*To Doris.*) For some people dating might be out of the question ... (*To Lucille.*) and for others it might be right. (*Quickly changing the subject.*) Those cookies look irresistible.

IDA. Please, help yourself.

(*HE takes a cookie and eats it.*)

LUCILLE. (*Pressing on.*) And which category do you fall into?

IDA. Lucille.

SAM. No, that's okay. For me ... I think it's time to move on. Sure I go pay my respects when I feel the need to but I also think I'm ready to start a new chapter. After all, what is life if not one chapter after another waiting to be written?

LUCILLE. Well put.

DORIS. (*To Sam.*) Before you take your pen out, Sam—don't you think there comes a time when you stop writing, when you find other things in life to enjoy, when you sit back and read?

SAM. As I said, I think you have to do what's right for you.

LUCILLE. Exactly. Some people are readers and some people are writers. (*To Sam.*) Me, I'm like you—a writer.

DORIS. (*Giving Lucille a look. Disgusted.*) I'm going to the bathroom.

(*SHE gets up and exits upstairs to the bathroom. There is a moment as the three are left not knowing where to take the conversation.*)

SAM. (*To Ida.*) You know, I'm looking at you and I swear you haven't aged a day since I know you.

IDA. Oh.

LUCILLE. Funny how time passes some **people right by. Now you take *me*. I don't look**

like I used to. People tell me I actually look
younger now than I did five years ago.

(*The tea KETTLE whistles. Pause.*)

IDA. (*To Lucille.*) Why don't *you* go make the
tea this time?
LUCILLE. And leave Sam here all by himself?

(*IDA gives her a look.*)

LUCILLE. I'll go make. (*SHE walks to the
kitchen and then turns back. Playfully.*) Now
behave yourselves you two. (*Exits.*)
SAM. She's quite a woman.
IDA. You think so?
SAM. I mean different, not shy.
IDA. No, Lucille never knew from shy.
SAM. It's strange but I keep thinking I've met
her before.
IDA. Could be. She makes friends very easily.
(*Pause.*) Funny running into you today.
SAM. And of all places.
IDA. Go figure.
SAM. (*Pause.*) So, I uh ... I hear Selma's
getting married again.
IDA. Yeah.
SAM. You going to the wedding?
IDA. Wouldn't miss it for the world. How
about you?
SAM. Sure. (*Pause. Nervously.*) Listen,
maybe since uh ... you're going and ... I'm going

... maybe you would ... you would want to take
one car ... You could ... go with me. I could
uh... drive you ... take you ... there ... to
Selma's wedding.

(*DORIS has entered unseen on the end of Sam's
line and has overheard this.*)

IDA. Sam, are you—? (*SHE sees Doris and
stops herself.*)

DORIS. Did I interrupt something?

IDA. (*Flustered.*) Sam and I were just talking
about Selma's wedding.

SAM. (*To Doris.*) You going to go?

DORIS. (*Sitting back down.*) I haven't
decided.

IDA. Of course she's going.

DORIS. (*Indifferently.*) Of course I'm going.

LUCILLE. (*Enters with the tea.*) Tea time.
(*Setting the tray down.*) So what did I miss?

DORIS. I'll let Ida tell you.

IDA. We were just discussing Selma's
wedding.

LUCILLE. Well I, for one, am looking
forward. (*Pouring the tea. To Sam.*) Milk?

SAM. Please. No sugar.

LUCILLE. (*To Sam.*) You going?

SAM. Yeah. I like Selma's weddings, they're
like reunions. Wait a minute. *That's* where I've
seen you before. Weren't you at Selma's last
wedding?

LUCILLE. I've been to all of them.

SAM. I thought you looked familiar. How do you like that. All this time and I didn't even recognize you.

LUCILLE. I looked different then. I was married.

DORIS. (*To Sam.*) Did you know Harry?

SAM. No.

DORIS. He died about a year and a half ago. Not long after Lou Green's unveiling. You remember Lou's unveiling don't you, Ida?

IDA. Yes.

DORIS. How upset Sylvia was.

IDA. Doris.

DORIS. How vulnerable.

IDA. Anyone for another cookie?

LUCILLE. (*To Doris. Fed up.*) I've had my limit for today.

SAM. I don't know how you could resist. They're absolutely wonderful, delicious. (*To Ida.*) I haven't tasted cookies this good since I don't know when.

IDA. It's nothing really. They're easy to make.

SAM. For you.

IDA. If you like I'll give you some you can take home.

SAM. I couldn't.

IDA. Please. I got plenty. I made to send to the kids but they still haven't sent the tin back from last time. Before you go I'll put some in a bag.

DORIS. What about the tea? Maybe you could put some in a container.

SAM. Tea is about the only thing I *can* make.

(*HE laughs. LUCILLE joins in then stops. HE continues laughing then stops awkwardly. Pause.*)

IDA. So is this a gorgeous day, or what?

LUCILLE. I got an idea. Why don't we go, the four of us, for a walk? (*Standing.*) What do you say, Doris? In honor of Abe. Sunday was his day for walking.

DORIS. (*Standing.*) You talked me into it.

IDA. Why don't you two go. I think I've had enough fresh air for one day.

SAM. I'll stay and finish tea. (*To Ida.*) That is if you don't mind.

IDA. Of course not.

DORIS. (*Sitting back down.*) I'm not in such a mood to go out anyway.

IDA. No, go. You two go. It'll do you good.

LUCILLE. (*Sitting back down.*) We'll stay. We'll play cards. (*To Sam.*) You've never seen "Ida the Greek" here play cards.

IDA. (*Firmly.*) I'm not in the mood for cards. You two go out. We'll talk tomorrow.

LUCILLE. (*Put off.*) O-kay.

(*SHE gets up and puts on her coat. DORIS looks at Ida.*)

DORIS. Our bags?

(IDA reaches under the couch and pulls out the two handbags.)

SAM. You keep your bags under the couch?
IDA. Some people use a vault. We've always used the couch.

(SHE hands Doris her bag then gives Lucille hers as DORIS puts on her coat.)

SAM. *(To Lucille.)* It was nice meeting you. *Again.*
LUCILLE. You too.
SAM. *(To Doris.)* Good to see you.
DORIS. *(Halfheartedly.)* Yeah.
SAM. I'm sorry if I caused any inconvenience.
DORIS. Well ...

(SHE turns away from him and heads for the door. IDA opens it.)

DORIS. Maybe we'll stop back in a little while.
IDA. No, you two enjoy yourselves. I'll call you tomorrow.
LUCILLE. Sure. We'll talk tomorrow.

(DORIS and LUCILLE exit. IDA closes the door behind them. SHE and SAM remain standing. There is a long moment as both feel a little awkward.)

IDA. Thank you for bringing over the livers. It was really very nice.

SAM. (*Bowing. Playfully gallant.*) It was nothing.

(*Pause.*)

IDA and SAM. So—

(*THEY laugh awkwardly.*)

IDA. (*Searching for a topic.*) So how's business?

SAM. Business is fine.

IDA. That's good.

SAM. Yeah. (*Pause. Searching.*) I've been having trouble with the help though.

IDA. No.

SAM. Yeah. I don't know, kids today they don't want to work so fast. Not like when we were young. Lately I've been thinking maybe I should sell the shop altogether.

IDA. You're kidding.

SAM. I keep asking myself why is it the kids I hire get younger and younger? The boy I got now looks to me like he's just out of diapers. But then I realize—the kids aren't getting younger. People don't get younger.

IDA. No.

SAM. (*Pause.*) You uh ... you have a beautiful home.

IDA. Thank you.

SAM. (*Re: the piano.*) You play?

IDA. A little. The children took lessons when they were young.

SAM. (*Looking at the many framed pictures on the piano.*) That's quite a family.

IDA. You happen to be looking at a woman who's five times a grandmother.

SAM. I've got my first on the way. Maybe you'll give me some pointers.

IDA. That's the best part. You don't need any. You just enjoy your grandchildren then sit back and smile as you watch them do everything to your children that your children did to you.

(*SAM laughs. His eyes focus on a particular picture. IDA notices.*)

IDA. That's Murry and me on our twenty-fifth anniversary. At the Concord.

SAM. Merna and I spent ours at Grossingers. I'll never forget it.

IDA. It's nice to have such good memories.

SAM. What good? We were playing mixed doubles on the tennis court, I had a heart attack at the net. My twenty-fifth anniversary present was a double bypass. (*Jokingly.*) At least it was something I could use.

(*IDA laughs. Pause. SHE reaches for his cup which is beside the pipe rack on top of the humidor.*)

SAM. (*Re: the pipe rack.*) Funny, I don't remember Murry as a smoker.

IDA. Mostly just after dinner. He didn't really smoke during the day. (*Pause. Changing the subject.*) You want some more tea?

SAM. Sit. I'll get it.

(*IDA sits on the couch as SAM refills the two cups. HE laughs to himself.*)

IDA. What?

SAM. I was just thinking about Sylvia Green. Doris made me think of her.

IDA. What's funny about that?

SAM. Well, you probably know. I mean, it's a small neighborhood.

IDA. (*Playing dumb.*) Know what?

(*SHE makes room for him on the couch but HE shies away and sits in the armchair.*)

SAM. Well ... we had this sort of date a while back.

IDA. Really?

SAM. If you could call it that. The whole thing was a fiasco. It all started at Lou's unveiling.

IDA. At the unveiling?

SAM. I know it sounds awful. It was all because of my son, Richie. After Merna died he didn't like the idea of my being on my own. He wouldn't stop buzjuring me to find someone. I think what he was really afraid of was that if he didn't find someone to move in with *me* I might move in with *him.* So he kept saying what I needed was a "friend." He loves to use that word "friend" for someone he thinks I should spend the rest of my life with. Anyway, after a few months I started thinking maybe I *could* find someone. So I started to go out. Each date was worse than the one before. Not that it was their fault. It was mine. Instead of looking at what a woman was like I kept looking at how unlike she was from Merna.

IDA. Not a fair thing to do.

SAM. No ... So my last date was with Sylvia. We were going out for dinner and I was determined to have a good time. I specifically picked a restaurant Merna and I had never been to—The Majestic on Jewel Avenue. You know it?

IDA. The Majestic ... isn't that where Sylvia's husband had his heart attack?

SAM. *That's* the place. Who knew? I pulled up in front of the restaurant and all of a sudden she starts screaming, "Take me away from here! Take me away from here!" We drove around for about an hour which gave her enough time to calm down about Lou and me enough time to start thinking about Merna. We both agreed that this was probably not the best time for us to continue our date. I took her home, apologized and said good night. We never tried again. I guess even without the fiasco we knew we wouldn't have been right for each other. We talk every now and then. She's a good woman and a nice friend. Oy, don't let Richie know I said that.

(*THEY laugh. Pause.*)

SAM. I shouldn't have been going out like that so soon after Merna died. I don't know what I was thinking. Funny, how after you lose someone, someone that close, you find yourself doing things you never even dreamed of, behaving in ways you never thought possible.

IDA. (*Confiding.*) I used to cook. Like a crazy woman, day and night. I don't think I left the kitchen for about a month after Murry passed away. I made meals that would put a French restaurant to shame. Five course dinners; roasts, chickens, breads, compotes, pies, you name it. Murry used to love my food. He used to say that my dinners were what brought him straight back home every day right after work. So after he died I kept making the dinners. I thought maybe if I made them, he—(*Stopping herself. Pause.*) I don't cook that much now. I still bake for the kids every once in a while.

SAM. You're close with them.

IDA. Oh yeah.

SAM. That's nice.

(*SHE holds out the pot of tea for him. HE gets up, lets her refill his cup and then sits beside her.*)

IDA. So, have you been going to the cemetery often lately?

SAM. Not really.

IDA. And what made you decide to go today?

SAM. This week would've been forty years Merna and I are married. I felt I should go.

IDA. (*Relieved.*) So you didn't go for any other reason.

SAM. For what other reason would I go to the cemetery?

IDA. Of course.

SAM. While I was there I was thinking back over all the years.

IDA. They do go by.

SAM. One day you're on your knee proposing, the next day you're standing at a grave remembering how nervous you were. (*Reflecting sadly.*) And somehow, before you know it, forty years have passed between the two days. (*Pause. Feeling very awkward.*) I should get going.

IDA. Wait. I'll get a bag, you'll take the rest of the cookies.

SAM. You don't have to.

IDA. It's my pleasure.

(*As IDA exits to the kitchen, SAM hastily gets his coat from the closet.*)

IDA. (*Offstage.*) So the affair will probably go until late.

SAM. (*Nervously.*) What affair?

(IDA reenters with a small plastic bag and puts in the remaining cookies as THEY talk.)

IDA. Selma's.

SAM. Oh ... I guess.

IDA. I'll tell Doris and Lucille to go themselves.

SAM. Were you all going to go together?

IDA. Yeah, but if you and I are—

SAM. No. I mean, I don't want to put them out.

IDA. I'm sure they won't mind.

SAM. *(Resolutely.)* Maybe it would be best for you to go with them.

IDA. *(Taken aback. Hurt.)* Oh ... Okay ... Sure ... I mean, it doesn't really matter. *(Hands him the bag.)*

SAM. Thank you.

(THEY walk to the door and stand looking at each other. The awkwardness builds.)

SAM. It was nice talking.

IDA. Yeah.

SAM. We'll have to do it again sometime.

IDA. Sure ... Well ... I'll see you when I see you.

SAM. Have a good night.

IDA. You too.

(SAM exits. IDA closes the door behind him then walks slowly back into the room. SHE begins

clearing up. After a moment the DOORBELL
rings. SHE walks back and opens the door.
It's Sam. HE stands in the doorway and speaks
quickly, in a business-like tone.)

SAM. Look, I could drive you there if you
want.
IDA. That would be nice.
SAM. Okay. Good night.

(*HE exits in a flash. IDA closes the door and*
smiles. SHE goes back to clearing up when the
BELL rings again. IDA opens the door. It's
Sam.)

SAM. (*Gathering up his nerve.*) Listen, I was
thinking ... since the wedding isn't for a while ...
how would you like ... I mean, how would you
feel... about maybe ... getting together Friday for
a movie?
IDA. Sounds good.
SAM. Yeah?
IDA. Yeah.
SAM. (*Braving ahead but still nervous.*) And
dinner. We'll see a movie and then have dinner.
Unless you would rather have dinner before. We
could have dinner first and then see the movie.
IDA. Either way sounds good.
SAM. Okay. Good night.
IDA. Good night.

(HE exits. IDA closes the door and smiles as the LIGHT fades out.)

Scene 4

The cemetery: Abe's plot. Late afternoon.
DORIS is sitting on her folding stool as SHE finishes trimming the ivy on Abe's grave.

DORIS. A lawsuit is what I should have. They should be paying *me* for the work I do around here. Every month the same thing.

(LUCILLE enters in her fur coat. SHE also wears a matching fur hat as SHE walks to Abe's grave.)

LUCILLE. Five thousand places we could've met and she picks the cemetery.
DORIS. (*Getting up.*) Hello, Lucille.

(THEY kiss.)

LUCILLE. I want you to know I would not have come here today if it weren't for this meeting.
DORIS. I know.
LUCILLE. Because I am through visiting Harry's grave.

DORIS. I think you made that point very clear last month.

LUCILLE. As long as it's clear. (*Proudly showing off the hat.*) So what do you think of the hat?

DORIS. Nice. Matches the coat.

LUCILLE. Guess how much.

DORIS. For something like that, if it's second-hand and you got a good price, with a little haggling you should've paid maybe, what, two hundred?

LUCILLE. (*Annoyed.*) What do you do, follow me into stores? (*Pause.*) The only reason I'm here is because I'm concerned for Ida.

DORIS. That's why I'm here.

LUCILLE. No, you're here because this is your favorite vacation spot. I'm here because I don't want to see her settle for the first man that comes along.

DORIS. Well, if she does you have only yourself to blame.

LUCILLE. *Me?*

DORIS. All your talk about not going to the cemetery. And she sees the way you behave.

LUCILLE. Good. Better she should follow in *my* footsteps than in yours.

DORIS. (*Pause.*) So, have you spoken to her lately?

LUCILLE. I have been out a lot this past month.

DORIS. A week can go by and I don't even know she's alive. At night she's out and during the day she's always got an excuse. Always a reason why she can't get together. I talk to her on the phone, it feels like a different person. Like everything we shared was just in my mind.

LUCILLE. (*Changing the subject.*) Are you sure Sam's coming?

DORIS. I'm sure.

LUCILLE. You told him the right place?

DORIS. I told him.

LUCILLE. And he said he'd be here?

DORIS. How many times are you going to ask?

LUCILLE. I just want to make sure he's coming, that's all. (*Pause.*) You told him four o'clock?

DORIS. (*Fed up.*) I told him midnight. I told him he should meet us at midnight, a week from tomorrow. On top of the Empire State building.

LUCILLE. Would've been better than here.

DORIS. (*Pause.*) You know what your going to say?

LUCILLE. What we discussed on the phone.

DORIS. (*Spotting SAM as HE approaches.*) Shh. Here he comes.

SAM. Hello Doris, Louise.

LUCILLE. *Lucille.*

SAM. Lucille, I'm sorry.

DORIS. Hello Sam.

SAM. So what's up? What did you want to talk to me about?

LUCILLE. (*To Doris.*) Tell Sam what you feel.

DORIS. What *I* feel? What happened to you?
LUCILLE. You're the one who brought it up.
SAM. What?
DORIS. Five minutes ago you were on my side, now you're on his?
LUCILLE. I'm not on anybody's side.
DORIS. Thank you, Miss Switzerland.
SAM. What sides? What are we talking about?
DORIS. We feel, *Lucille* and I, that uh ... that you should stop doing something you're doing.
SAM. (*To Doris.*) I've done something to you?
DORIS. Not to me.
SAM. (*To Lucille.*) To you?
LUCILLE. No, but I really haven't given you much of a chance.
SAM. To who then?
DORIS. To Ida.
SAM. (*Stunned.*) Ida?
LUCILLE. Yes.
SAM. What could I have possibly done to Ida?

(*DORIS looks to LUCILLE who finally takes the lead. SHE begins to pace. A lecture is imminent.*)

LUCILLE. Sam, a woman's heart is a funny thing. Am I right, Doris?
DORIS. Yes, Lucille.
LUCILLE. A woman's heart is a very fragile thing. Right or wrong, Doris?
DORIS. Right, Lucille.
LUCILLE. A woman's heart—

DORIS. It's gonna be *dark* soon, Lucille.

LUCILLE. And after a woman's husband dies her heart breaks. It breaks into many pieces. And when she finally tries to put those pieces back together again she finds that a whole half of her heart is missing, gone, buried six feet under a headstone with her husband's name on it.

(*DORIS begins to weep.*)

LUCILLE. She then has to find another half, a new half to her broken heart. And she does that by ... playing the field.

DORIS. What?!

SAM. What does all this have to do with me?

DORIS. What Lucille is trying to say, *in the worst way possible,* is that what's going on with you and Ida is no good.

SAM. What are you talking about?

DORIS. What am I talking about? I'm talking about this whole past month.

SAM. We've been having a wonderful time together. We've seen a few movies, gone out for dinner, saw a musical.

DORIS. Sam, Ida and I have been coming here together every month for almost three years and now since the two of you have started with this ... this ... *dating* she can't face her husband.

SAM. She told me last week that she just thought it would be good to not go as often.

DORIS. What do you expect her to say? She's afraid. She feels tremendous guilt.

LUCILLE. That's very true.

DORIS. And on top of that you're planning on taking her to Selma's wedding where she'll have to face *everyone*. All her friends. Everyone who saw her last time with Murry. What do you think that's going to do to her?

LUCILLE. And to you. Taking a woman to a wedding is no small matter.

SAM. But we have nothing to hide.

DORIS. All I'm saying is that going to Selma's wedding together is wrong. What if God forbid it was you in this cemetery? God forbid, you should only live and be well, but just suppose it was reversed. Do you think Merna would be showing up at Selma's wedding with a man? Especially someone you both knew. Not only are you defaming the memory of Merna and Murry, but it also shows no consideration for Ida.

SAM. Did she say this to you?

DORIS. When you've been friends as long as we have, words aren't necessary.

LUCILLE. We see it in her behavior.

DORIS. She's upset, confused.

SAM. I don't want to do anything to upset her.

DORIS. Then let her go to Selma's wedding with us the way she originally wanted to.

LUCILLE. (*Suddenly*.) And then you can come and take all of us.

(*DORIS gives her a look.*)

LUCILLE. (*To Doris.*) That way it won't seem so much like a date.

DORIS. (*Ignoring her. To Sam.*) It's going to be hard enough for her as it is. Going to a wedding, being a bridesmaid, not having Murry there. That's an awful lot to deal with, Sam.

SAM. I don't want to make things any more difficult for her.

LUCILLE. So we'll all go together.

(*DORIS gives her a look again.*)

SAM. You know Ida better than I do. If that's what you think then okay.

DORIS. I knew you'd understand.

SAM. I should get going. I'll uh ... I'll see you in two weeks.

DORIS. Yeah.

(*HE begins walking away.*)

DORIS. And Sam.

(*HE turns back.*)

DORIS. Think about what you're doing. Not just the wedding. The whole thing. You, Ida, Merna. Are you sure it's right?

(*HE looks at her a moment then turns and leaves.*)

LUCILLE. So I think we did pretty good.

DORIS. (*Annoyed. Imitating Lucille.*) "And you can come and take all of us."

LUCILLE. Why not?

DORIS. Because it wasn't necessary. And you had to start with the playing in the field again.

LUCILLE. It's what she should be doing.

DORIS. You're out of your mind, you know that?

LUCILLE. Why, because I don't think she should spend the rest of her life polishing Murry's headstone?

DORIS. I polished Abe's headstone *twice*. Twice in four years!

LUCILLE. You clean his headstone more often than I clean my dining room table!

DORIS. Now you know why we never come to your house for dinner. (*Pause.*) What are we arguing? The important thing is that we put an end to this whole Sam business. (*Pause.*) So, you going to go over to Harry while you're here?

LUCILLE. Eh, what the hell. He bought me the hat. The least I could do is show it to him.

DORIS. Come on. I'll go with you. I haven't said hello for a while. (*SHE places a stone on Abe's headstone.*)

LUCILLE. (*Suddenly becoming reflective.*) You know, Harry always used to say I had a hat face. "On any other woman," he'd say "a hat is just a hat. But on you it's the tops."

(*THEY gather their things and begin walking during the following.*)

DORIS. Abe wasn't a hat lover.

LUCILLE. No?

DORIS. No. Long flowing hair was all he wanted. You remember how long my hair used to be.

LUCILLE. Sure.

DORIS. Those were the days, ey Lucille? You in the Paris hats, me with the long red curls and Ida with the clips.

LUCILLE. (*Smiling, remembering.*) Clips.

DORIS. She was always crazy about hair clips.

LUCILLE. We were quite a threesome.

DORIS. Yeah.

(*THEY exit as the curtain comes down on the cemetery.*)

ACT II

Scene 1

IDA's living room.
A suitcase lays open on one of the chairs, a make-up mirror has been set up on a table, and an ironing board stands off to the side. Murry's pipe rack is gone.
AT RISE: DORIS is ironing her dress. IDA enters holding a scarf around her hair.

IDA. What do you think? (*SHE pulls off the scarf revealing a new hair cut.*)

DORIS. Looks fine.

IDA. I don't want fine.

DORIS. What's wrong with fine?

IDA. Fine is fine. It's not sensational.

DORIS. What's so important you have to look *sensational?*

IDA. It's Selma's wedding.

DORIS. I would hardly call that a special occasion.

IDA. There has to be a reason for me to want to look good?

DORIS. Good, no. Sensational, yes.

IDA. There's no reason.

DORIS. There's no reason. You've been running around here like a schoolgirl before a prom and there's no reason.

IDA. All right, all right ... I just wanted to look good—

DORIS. *Sensational.*

IDA. *Sensational* ... so I could ... for Sam.

DORIS. (*Disappointed.*) For Sam.

IDA. Yes. I didn't want to tell you 'cause I didn't think you would understand.

DORIS. (*Pause.*) So the two of you have still been seeing a lot of each other.

IDA. Well, we were. We were going to the movies on Friday nights—

DORIS. Canasta night.

IDA. You're still not upset about that.

DORIS. Don't be silly.

IDA. But lately I haven't got to see him much. He said he had a cold last week and this week he's been very tired from work. He's been having trouble with the help.

DORIS. I see.

IDA. But I keep wondering if maybe something's wrong.

DORIS. Has he said something's wrong?

IDA. No, but he just doesn't seem the same when I talk to him. I don't know. Maybe it's me. Maybe I'm just not used to this whole thing.

DORIS. Look how upset you're getting. Tell me, is it worth it ...? Listen, tomorrow we'll go to the cemetery. You'll forget all about Sam. Supposed to be a beautiful day tomorrow. And

maybe after, we'll go for a little lunch. My treat.
What do you think?
IDA. You don't understand.

(*SHE runs upstairs to the bedroom. The
DOORBELL rings. DORIS opens the door.
LUCILLE enters, wearing her fur coat and hat,
carrying a valise, hat box and shoulder bag.*)

LUCILLE. Hello.
DORIS. Hello.

(*LUCILLE puts down her things. THEY kiss
cheek to cheek.*)

LUCILLE. I like your hair. Looks good
DORIS. Thank you. I thought I'd try
something a little different.
LUCILLE. Where's Ida?
DORIS. In the bedroom.
LUCILLE. (*Calling upstairs.*) Hello, Ida.
IDA. (*Offstage.*) Hello, Lucille.
LUCILLE. (*To Doris.*) Has she said anything
about us going with her?
DORIS. No.
LUCILLE. It'll be fun to all stay here tonight.
Like a slumber party.
DORIS. I like being in my own bed.
LUCILLE. Why, what happens there?
DORIS. I wouldn't expect you to understand.

(*LUCILLE pulls out a fur hand muff from under valise. SHE puts her hands in the muff and strikes a pose.*)

LUCILLE. (*Proudly, re the muff.*) So what do you think?

DORIS. Nice.

LUCILLE. Who would believe I'd be able to find such a perfect match? Exact same color as the hat and coat.

DORIS. All you need now is mink shoes.

LUCILLE. (*Defiantly.*) All right ... *Guess how much.*

DORIS. What's the difference?

LUCILLE. No, I want you to guess. Come on.

DORIS. For something like that, if it was on sale and you got a good price, with a little haggling you should've paid maybe what, a hundred twenty-five?

LUCILLE. (*Beaming! Savoring the moment.*) *Forty-five dollars.*

DORIS. (*Stunned.*) You're kidding.

LUCILLE. I got the receipt!

DORIS. (*Impressed.*) That's some buy. (*Feeling the muff.*) It's not real.

LUCILLE. What are you talking about?

DORIS. I thought it was real. If you told me it wasn't real I would have said about forty-five dollars.

LUCILLE. Of course it's real!

DORIS. I know mink. That's not real. Real you can pull out the fur. (*Pulling the fur.*) This doesn't come out.

LUCILLE. It's well made.

DORIS. I don't care how well made it is, it's not real.

(*IDA enters carrying her bridesmaid's dress and a pair of matching shoes.*)

LUCILLE. (*To Doris.*) You keep quiet. (*Going over to Ida.*) Ida, what do you think of the muff?

IDA. (*Lays her dress over a chair and puts the shoes on the floor.*) Beautiful. (*Feeling it.*) Nice, soft, well made. If I didn't know I'd think it was real.

DORIS. Thank you.

(*LUCILLE marches off and hangs her furs in the closet.*)

IDA. What's with her?

DORIS. She thought it was real.

LUCILLE. (*Testily.*) I didn't think it was real. I was just testing. (*Pointing to the coffee table.*) I'll set up over there.

(*SHE takes out her make-up and arranges an area for herself on the coffee table. SHE then sits on the couch and begins putting on her face.*
IDA puts in her new contact lenses.)

IDA. Selma called me yesterday and said this affair's going to be the best yet.

LUCILLE. I think the affairs get better each time. The marriages get worse but the affairs get better.

IDA. You remember the second one?

LUCILLE. Sure. The bakery guy.

IDA. Nat Stein, from Nat's noshery.

DORIS. What an affair that was. An eight course dinner and seven of them were desserts.

LUCILLE. It took me two months to lose the weight I gained that night.

DORIS. To this day I can't look at a canoli without getting sick to my stomach.

IDA. Well we won't have to worry about that this time. This Ed fella is in the fruit business.

LUCILLE. Fruit?

DORIS. Oy, am I going to have gas.

LUCILLE. She went from cakes to fruit? What kind of advancement is that?

IDA. (*To Lucille, indicating make-up*.) Can I use a little?

LUCILLE. Of course.

IDA. (*Holding some eye shadow up to her face*.) The green eye shadow?

DORIS. Sure.

IDA. You don't think it's too much?

LUCILLE. You'll knock 'em dead.

IDA. Dead, I got.

(*DORIS makes a fist then releases it. SHE does this a few times*.)

LUCILLE. You okay?

DORIS. It's nothing. Every once in a while I get a pain, shoots through the arm.

IDA. I get it in the fingers sometimes in the morning. I find if I wear the copper bracelet it helps.

DORIS. I've tried. Doesn't do anything except maybe I get a little better reception on my TV.

LUCILLE. Harry used to get it bad when it was going to rain. Never failed. The weather man could say tomorrow was going to be nice and sunny. If Harry's hand hurt I took an umbrella.

DORIS. ... Funny, last time we were at Selma's wedding we all had husbands. I hope she's paying by the head.

IDA. Every affair there's fewer and fewer people. I wonder who'll be missing from this one.

LUCILLE. Hopefully, some wives.

IDA. Lucille.

LUCILLE. (*To Ida.*) So what time is Sam coming to pick us up?

IDA. ... I don't know.

LUCILLE. What do you mean you don't know?

IDA. Last time we spoke he said five o'clock but we haven't seen each other for a while. He could have forgotten.

LUCILLE. Well haven't you spoken to him recently?

IDA. No.

LUCILLE. And you haven't seen him at all?

IDA. Not the past couple of weeks.

(*LUCILLE shares a look with Doris.*)

IDA. He says he's just been very tired. I don't know. I keep trying to figure out if maybe I did something wrong the last time we went out. We had such a nice night. He came to the door with flowers. (*To Doris.*) When's the last time you were given flowers?

DORIS. Abe's funeral.

LUCILLE. Harry used to come home with them all the time. That's how I knew he was cheating. The younger the woman the bigger the bouquet. Once I got two dozen roses. I figured that's it. He's up for statutory rape.

IDA. Sam brought tulips. Yellow tulips. They were beautiful.

LUCILLE. Well maybe you should call, make sure he's coming.

IDA. I don't think I should.

LUCILLE. Then I'll call. (*Gets up and goes over to the phone.*)

DORIS. So if he doesn't come we'll drive ourselves.

LUCILLE. Don't be silly. Why should we go unescorted? (*To Ida.*) What's his number?

IDA. Lucille, I think it's a little forward to call.

LUCILLE. (*Dialing.*) You can never be too forward. (*On the phone.*) Hello, in Forest Hills, could I please have the number of a Samuel Katz

... (*Covering the receiver. To Ida and Doris.*)
Wants to know if it's with a "C." (*To the
operator.*) With a "K." Starts with a "K," ends
with a "Z." (*To Ida and Doris.*) A Jewish girl
she's not. (*To the operator.*) Sam-u-el ... Just like
it sounds. Starts with "S"and go *straight* to "L" ...
That's it (*Writing down the number then again to
the operator.*) Thank you and have a safe trip back
to earth. (*SHE clears the line and then dials the
number.*) Hello, Sam ... It's me ... *Lucille* ...
Fine, how are you ...? Glad to hear it ... Ah ha ...
ah ha... ah ha ... okay ... of course. Goodbye.
(*Hangs up the phone.*)

    IDA. Well?

    LUCILLE. He was just leaving.

    IDA. (*Panicked.*) Now?! Look what I look
like!

    DORIS. We better get a move on.

    LUCILLE. (*Grabbing her things.*) I'll get
dressed in your bedroom. I need a full length
mirror. (*Heading upstairs.*) Wait 'til you see what
I've put together.

(*SHE exits to the bedroom. IDA and DORIS look
    at each other.*)

    IDA. I think she said she's wearing shoulder
pads.

    DORIS. Under something or by themselves?

    IDA. Well, she's got to wear the dress Selma
picked out.

(*THEY begin getting dressed and continue throughout the scene. THEY wear identical bridesmaid's dresses.*)

DORIS. Funny, I've never been to one of Selma's weddings without Abe. I feel a little nervous.

IDA. Me too.

DORIS. It's going to be strange seeing all the old faces ... the friends, the couples.

IDA. Murry used to love to make up stories about everyone there. Just for me, I mean. I'd point out a couple and he'd make up a funny story about them—how they met, how they argue ... I used to laugh.

DORIS. All Abe wanted was to be on the dance floor. All night he could dance.

IDA. *Me* you're telling? He pulled me up more than once.

DORIS. The cha-cha, that's what we loved. The cha-cha-cha.

IDA. (*Pause.*) You going to dance tonight?

DORIS. Me? I don't think ... I don't think I could.

IDA. You afraid?

DORIS. Of what?

IDA. Of dancing.

DORIS. Don't be ridiculous. What's to be afraid? I just don't think I'll be in the mood, that's all.

IDA. How could you know now if—

DORIS. Enough already with the dancing. What's so important?

IDA. Nothing. Here. (*SHE gives Doris her back so she can do her up. Pause.*)

DORIS. *You* going to dance?

IDA. If someone asks.

DORIS. But you ... you want to.

IDA. If my feet don't object why should *I?*

(*THEY both turn so Ida can zip up Doris.*)

DORIS. You still love to dance, don't you?

(*IDA smiles.*)

DORIS. You uh ... you want to dance with Sam?

IDA. If he asks.

DORIS. And it wouldn't bother you it wasn't Murry.

IDA. Doris, it can't be Murry. And what should I do? I'm standing, the music's playing, and Murry's not on the dance floor. What should I do?

DORIS. Go back to your table.

IDA. (*Turning Doris to face her.*) Listen to me, Doris. For you it's enough to have your friends, family, children, and live alone. Me, I can't do it. I need to *be* with someone, to *give* to someone. That afternoon, when you and Lucille left and Sam and I were alone, I came alive. I felt awkward, nervous, excited—my heart was *pounding.* For the first time since Murry died I felt *alive*. And yes, part of me still feels miserable for feeling that good. But I'm not going to give in. I'm not going to spend the rest of my life feeling guilty for wanting to be touched, to be held by someone who isn't Murry.

(There is a long moment as the two WOMEN look at each other. Doris doesn't know how to respond. SHE turns and begins putting her make-up and things in her small suitcase.)

DORIS. You know, I was thinking, when I go to the cemetery tomorrow, of maybe telling them to take up the ivy from Abe's plot and replace it with wood chips. I figure that way it's good all year 'round and ... and I won't have to worry if they're watering and ... and the wood chips I think look nice.

IDA. I'm not going tomorrow, Doris.

DORIS. Did I say anything about you going? I didn't hear your name mentioned.

IDA. Why don't you try one month not going to the cemetery?

DORIS. Ida ... You do what's right for you. I'll do what's right for me.

IDA. Okay.

(THEY hug. The DOORBELL rings.)

IDA. Oh my God! He's here!
DORIS. Ida.

IDA. Where are my shoes?

DORIS. There's something ... something I think I should tell you.

IDA. (*Running around, looking.*) My *shoes.*

DORIS. (*Pointing next to the couch.*) There ... Listen to me. Lucille and I did something—

IDA. How do I look? I look okay?

DORIS. You look ... *sensational.*

IDA. (*Aware of Doris's choice of the word.*) Thank you.

DORIS. Listen to me—

IDA. (*Grabbing her things.*) Oh, God, my jewelry. I don't have any of my jewelry.

DORIS. Ida—

IDA. (*Frantic.*) You open the door. (*Running upstairs. Excited.*) I *can't.*

(*SHE exits to the bedroom. DORIS goes to the door, straightens herself out, and opens it. SAM enters in a dark suit and bow tie. He does look handsome.*)

SAM. Hello, Doris.
DORIS. Hello, Sam.

(*Suddenly a WOMAN steps in beside Sam. DORIS is quite taken aback.*)

DORIS. *Mildred?*
MILDRED. Hello, Doris.
DORIS. I wasn't aware that you were coming with us.

MILDRED. Well, I was supposed to go with George and Elaine but Sam and I were out having dinner last night and I was telling him how the only thing worse than going to a wedding alone is going as a third wheel and he said he wasn't going with anyone either. I mean, he's driving you and Ida and Lucille but he wasn't *going* with anyone. So he asked me to go with him. How could I resist?

DORIS. Of course.

SAM. She didn't want to go with George and Elaine.

DORIS. (*To Sam.*) It's nice to see you working on a new chapter so quickly.

MILDRED. (*To Sam.*) I just hope those are your dancing shoes you're wearing because I have no intention of letting you leave the dance floor.

(*SHE puts her arm through his. Just then IDA comes down the stairs. SHE sees Mildred and freezes.*)

MILDRED. Hi, Ida.

IDA. (*Pause. Stunned.*) Mildred.

DORIS. (*Gently.*) Mildred's going with us. Well, actually, she's *going* with Sam but she's *coming* with us.

SAM. (*Awkwardly.*) Hello, Ida.

IDA. (*Trying to conceal the hurt.*) ... Hello, Sam.

MILDRED. (*Noticing the dresses.*) So you girls are bridesmaids this time.

IDA. Yeah.

MILDRED. I haven't been asked yet. Maybe her next wedding.

(*SHE laughs. NO ONE joins in.*)

SAM. (*To Ida.*) You look very nice. (*Also to Doris.*) You both do.

IDA. Thank you. (*Pause.*) Well, why don't we sit down?

(*SAM takes off his hat and coat. MILDRED gives him her back indicating that he should remove her fur wrap. HE does. THEY sit.*)

MILDRED. So, I hear this Ed fella Selma's marrying is loaded. Have either of you met him?

DORIS. No.

IDA. Not yet.

DORIS. It all happened rather quickly.

MILDRED. I know. First she was with Arnold then before any of us knew it she was with Ed.

DORIS. It's amazing how fast some people find replacements, wouldn't you say?

IDA. (*Pause. To Sam.*) So I ... haven't seen you for a while.

SAM. I've been busy.

DORIS. I'll say.

MILDRED. (*To Ida.*) Can you believe he's selling the butcher shop?

IDA. I didn't know.

MILDRED. (*To Sam.*) Oh, I'm sorry. Did you not want people to know yet?

SAM. It's no secret. I put it up for sale last week.

IDA. Why?

MILDRED. That's exactly what I said.

SAM. I think it's time.

IDA. What will you do?

SAM. I'm not sure yet.

MILDRED. Well, I can't imagine going anywhere else.

SAM. There's Irving's place over on Queens Boulevard. He's got a great little shop.

MILDRED. It just won't be the same. (*To Ida.*) Am I wrong?

IDA. (*Turns away, unable to even look at her anymore.*) I don't know what's taking Lucille. (*Shouting to the bedroom.*) Lucille, you ready?

LUCILLE. (*Offstage.*) Be down in a minute. Sam here?

DORIS. He's here Lucille.

LUCILLE. Hello, Sam.

SAM. Hello, Lucille.

(*Long pause.*)

IDA and SAM. So ...

SAM. Go ahead.

IDA. No, you go. It really wasn't anything important.

SAM. I was just going to say that uh ... I uh ... I hope we don't hit too much traffic.

IDA. Yeah. (*Pause. Searching.*) Can I get anybody something to drink?

DORIS. No.

SAM. Not for me.

MILDRED. (*Feeling uncomfortable.*) Actually, I think I could use a little water.

(*IDA starts getting up.*)

MILDRED. You stay. I'll get it. Just point me in the right direction.

IDA. (*Pointing.*) The glasses are above the sink.

(*MILDRED exits. There is a long awkward silence.*)

DORIS. (*Calling upstairs.*) Lucille, we're going to be late!

LUCILLE. Coming.

DORIS. I can't understand how it could take a woman who wears so little so long to get dressed.

LUCILLE. (*Very nonchalantly saunters down the steps.*) Has anybody seen my lipstick?

(*SHE looks around the room for her lipstick as SAM, IDA and DORIS take in the sight before them:*
LUCILLE is wearing the same dress as Ida and Doris but she has remodeled it for a sexier

look, adding a slit that is nearly as high as the new bust line is low. Some dresses cling to the body, Lucille's clutches. If her breasts were pushed up any higher they would be in her mouth. The amount of jewelry on her hands makes one wonder how she could point without tipping over. Finally, she has capped off the outfit with a full blond wig.)

LUCILLE. I know I put it down somewhere ... Here it is. (*SHE begins applying the lipstick when SHE notices everyone is staring at her.*) What? (*Knowingly.*) Don't tell me. (*Pointing to a tiny brooch on her breast.*) You think the brooch is too much.

IDA. The brooch I like.

DORIS. Keep the brooch.

SAM. What brooch?

LUCILLE. Men. Never notice anything. (*To Ida and Doris.*) So what do you think?

IDA. Of what?

LUCILLE. Of the new look. Is it me or what?

DORIS. That's what I'm trying to figure out.

LUCILLE. Oh come on. I don't look that different. I thought the wig would be fun. You've got to admit it's a knockout.

DORIS. Words could not express how knocked out I think you look.

LUCILLE. Tonight, no one is going to say that Harry Rubin's widow has given up on life!

IDA. Tonight, no one is going to *recognize* Harry Rubin's widow.

LUCILLE. Exactly! (*To Sam.*) And you, Mr. Katz, if you play your cards right, just might be able to get a dance.

(*MILDRED enters from the kitchen.*)

LUCILLE. (*Shocked.*) Mildred?
MILDRED. (*Pause. Barely recognizing her.*) Lucille?
LUCILLE. What are you doing here?
MILDRED. Going to the wedding. (*To Sam, indicating her fur wrap.*) Sam.

(*HE gets the wrap and puts it around her.*)

DORIS. Sam, being the gentleman that he is, offered to take Mildred.

(*LUCILLE looks to IDA who forces a smile as THEY all put on their coats.*)

LUCILLE. How thoughtful. (*To Sam.*) Are we picking anyone else up on the way?
SAM. (*Smiling, trying to ease the tension.*) I think the car's full.
LUCILLE. It's a good thing you don't drive a bus.

(*SHE opens the door and exits. DORIS follows leaving Mildred standing between IDA and SAM who are now looking at each other.*)

MILDRED. Sam.

(*HE escorts her out. IDA takes a deep breath, exits and closes the door behind her as the LIGHTS fade out.*)

Scene 2

Ida's living room.
It is 2:00 A.M. and the room is dark except for a faint LIGHT creeping in through the windows from the street lamps outside.
The three WOMEN can be heard giggling and chattering outside. THEY are all fairly drunk and trying, without much success, to unlock the front door. Eventually, the door is flung open and the WOMEN stumble in. IDA searches for the light switch as the door slams shut.)

LUCILLE. My coat! My coat's caught in the door! I'm stuck! Put on the light!

IDA. I can't find the switch.

DORIS. I'll get the doorknob.

LUCILLE. ... That is *not* the doorknob!

IDA. The switch was right here on the wall when I left.

DORIS. I'll get the coat.

LUCILLE. Don't you dare!

IDA. (*Laughing*.) Somebody stole the light switch.

DORIS. I got the coat.

LUCILLE. That's my dress! Leave it! I'll get the door.

(*The door opens and shuts.*)

IDA. I found the switch!

(*The LIGHTS go on and we see the women clearly for the first time. THEY are all a bit disheveled; hair a mess, clothes a little wrinkled, and Lucille's wig is severely lopsided. Most noticeable, however, is the fact that Doris is missing.*)

IDA. Where's Doris?

(*The DOORBELL rings. IDA goes to open the door. LUCILLE stops her.*)

LUCILLE. Who is it?

DORIS. (*From outside.*) I don't think that's funny, Lucille.

LUCILLE. Doris, is that you?

DORIS. Yes, it's me!

LUCILLE. What are you doing out this late at night?

(*LUCILLE and IDA laugh as LUCILLE opens the door. DORIS enters.*)

DORIS. (*To Lucille.*) I hope next time you rip your coat to shreds!

(*IDA bursts out laughing, followed by LUCILLE, then DORIS.*)

IDA. Somebody give me a hand with this.

(*From behind the armchair, IDA and DORIS lift up an enormous flower arrangement with a banner reading "Selma and Ed Bonfigliano." THEY carry it to one of the tables as LUCILLE hangs up her coat.*)

DORIS. We've really got to stop drinking at Selma's weddings. We could become alcoholics.
IDA. You think this one will last?
LUCILLE. Judging from the looks of him, I think even if it lasts 'til death do they part, she's only got a few months.

(*THEY laugh. DORIS hangs her coat and Ida's in the closet. LUCILLE takes her muff and walks over to the armchair.*)

IDA. Who wants some tea?
LUCILLE. Forget the tea. Let's have some more wine.
DORIS. I've had enough.
LUCILLE. Tonight we're having *more* than enough!

IDA. I don't have any wine.
LUCILLE. I took from the affair.

(*SHE pulls out a bottle of wine from inside her muff. IDA gets glasses as DORIS sits on the couch.*)

DORIS. Oy, I almost forgot. I got cake. (*Opens her bag and takes out a few pieces of cake that have been wrapped in napkins.*)
LUCILLE. Terrific. We'll have wine and cake. (*Pours three glasses.*)
DORIS. And cookies. I took also some cookies. (*SHE pulls out a napkin filled with cookies.*)
IDA. They were good cookies.
DORIS. I also got some of those tiny chicken wings. (*SHE pulls out another large napkined package.*) I couldn't get the dip. I should've brought a container.
LUCILLE. Wine, cake, cookies, chicken wings. What more could we want?
DORIS. Fruit! (*Pulling each fruit out of her bag.*) A banana ... two oranges ... an apple ... some grapes ... a kiwi ... and ... I don't know what this was.
LUCILLE. (*Raising her glass.*) A toast. To us!
IDA. (*Raising her glass.*) To us.
DORIS. (*Raising her glass.*) Why not?

(*THEY drink.*)

DORIS. And here's to Selma Bonfigliano!
IDA and LUCILLE. Selma Bonfigliano!

(*THEY drink.*)

IDA. And here's to Mildred. (*SHE drinks.*)
DORIS. (*Changing the subject.*) Who's having cake?
LUCILLE. A sliver.
IDA. It's lucky we had her along. Who else would've talked the whole car ride?

(*DORIS gives a big piece of cake to Lucille.*)

LUCILLE. That's to you a sliver?
DORIS. Sue me.
IDA. Talk, talk, talk. I don't know how anybody puts up with it.
DORIS. (*Handing Ida a piece of cake.*) Forget about it.
IDA. (*Sitting down.*) And did you ever see anyone dance like she did? I mean, I really think she made a spectacle of herself. A real spectacle. Don't you think she made a spectacle? I think she made a spectacle. But I guess men like that.
LUCILLE. Then let's us make a spectacle. How about some music?
IDA. Great idea. (*SHE gets up and runs over to the stereo cabinet. Searching through some records.*) Let's see.

(*DORIS gets up and approaches Lucille.*)

LUCILLE. What?
DORIS. What? Look in the mirror you'll see what. (*Straightens Lucille's wig.*)

(*DORIS sits back down. IDA puts on a record. It is a cha-cha.*)

DORIS. (*Smiling.*) Oohh.

(*IDA stares across the room into Doris's eyes. SHE then starts toward her.*)

DORIS. What? What are you ...?
LUCILLE. You gotta dance, Doris.
DORIS. Oh ... Oh no. No, no.
IDA. Come on. Neither of us danced all night.
DORIS. I couldn't even—

(*IDA grabs her and the two WOMEN cha-cha around the room as LUCILLE watches.*)

LUCILLE. Look at the ladies go!
DORIS. Oy! ... Oy!
IDA. Feels great, ey Doris?!
DORIS. Would feel better if you weren't such a lousy dancer.
IDA. *You* try following a rotten partner.
DORIS. I *am*.

(*THEY break away and start laughing.*)

LUCILLE. (*Getting up.*) Neither of you knows how to dance. *This* is how a cha-cha is done!
DORIS. (*To Ida re Lucille.*) The maven.

(*IDA and DORIS watch as LUCILLE dances alone around the room.*)

IDA. That's to you a cha-cha? *This* is a cha-cha!

(*IDA dances alone around the room. DORIS watches them both.*)

DORIS. I've never seen so many left feet. Where's the grace? Where's the style?

(*DORIS dances alone around the room. All three WOMEN are now cha-chaing around the room. Each is dancing as if with her husband.*)

IDA. Brings back memories, ey Doris?
DORIS. The cruises, the Catskills, Roseland.
LUCILLE. Boy, could Harry move me around.
IDA. They used to clear the floor when the magnificent six got up to dance.
LUCILLE. What did you expect, the way you swung your arms.

(*DORIS stops and begins rubbing her chest.*)

IDA. You okay?

DORIS. I knew I shouldn't have eaten that last mango.

LUCILLE. I'll get a little milk.

DORIS. Thanks.

(LUCILLE dances off to the kitchen.)

IDA. Just relax.

(DORIS sits on the couch. IDA turns down the music. It continues softly under their dialogue.)

IDA. Better?

DORIS. Yeah. (*Pause.*) A lot of people were missing from that wedding.

IDA. Don't.

DORIS. I looked for faces.

IDA. Probably too much of a schlep for some people.

DORIS. I looked for Abe. And you know the funny thing? I saw him ... I saw him eating, walking, dancing ... I actually saw him dancing. And the first question that popped into my mind was why aren't I dancing with him? That was the first thing I thought of. Why aren't I with him ...? That ever happen to you? You ever see Murry?

IDA. You mean picture him doing something?

DORIS. No, *see* him. You turn around and he's there.

IDA. Sometimes ... I remember once I came home one afternoon, late. It must have been around five, six ... and I could have sworn I saw

Murry over there. Just as I was coming in. I could have sworn I saw him sitting in his chair.

LUCILLE. (*Enters with a glass. Handing it to Doris.*) Here's the milk.

DORIS. Thank you.

IDA. Funny thing was I saw him the way he looked when we first started dating, just before he went off to the war. With thick, wavy black hair. Back then he had some head of hair. Dubrow's restaurant. That was where we met. A mutual friend, Ruth Cutler, set us up. She was with her boyfriend, I forgot his name, and they brought Murry along. Murry and her boyfriend went to school together. The whole meal I couldn't take my eyes off him. I don't know how I didn't poke myself in the face with my fork. And I remember thinking he didn't have any interest in me. Murry was like that back then. Very cool. The next day I get a call from Ruth. Murry had given her his number and told her to have *me* call *him*. What nerve, I thought. So I called. I said "Hello, this is Ida. My number is Rivington 7-6207. If you want to talk to me, call me." I hung up and prayed. Sure enough, he called back. And the rest, as they say, is history.

DORIS. First time I saw Abe was in my father's store. I was nineteen, working behind the counter. He was in the second aisle over. I couldn't see his face but I see through the bottom shelf that he's wearing an old pair of pants and there's a big hole in the top of his right shoe. This was definitely not a boy with money so I keep a careful watch. All of a sudden he bends down, grabs a loaf of bread, and I see he's putting it inside his jacket. I run over and stand behind him. He gets up, looks me straight in the eyes ... I felt my heart pound. I don't know what came over me. As he started to walk out I yelled at the top of my lungs "Crook! Crook!" It was the only way I could think of keeping him there. And it worked. My father ran out and grabbed him. A month and a half later we were married ... My father always used to joke "This is my son-in-law the crook. First he stole my bread ..." (*SHE smiles.*)

IDA. (*To Lucille.*) How about you? You ever see Harry?

LUCILLE. I didn't see him that much when he was alive. Why should I see him when he's dead?

IDA. What about when you're with other men?

LUCILLE. What do you mean?

IDA. You know, when you're in bed, having... you know, sex with another man. Do you ever see Harry ... in your mind?

LUCILLE. No.

IDA. Not even once it didn't happen?

LUCILLE. (*Getting up.*) No. (*Shutting off the record player.*) Who's having some more wine?

DORIS. I don't believe you.

LUCILLE. Why, were you there?

DORIS. I couldn't *dance* with another man without thinking of Abe.

LUCILLE. First of all, you couldn't do *anything* without thinking of Abe—

DORIS. Not true.

LUCILLE. And second of all, you're not me. So don't tell me what I think and don't think! (*To Ida.*) You having some more wine?

IDA. I've had enough.

LUCILLE. Of course. Everybody's had enough. Always enough. Don't go too far. Don't have too much. Just enough! Well I've had enough and I'm having more. (*SHE pours herself another glass.*)

IDA. Lucille.

LUCILLE. When you die you should have it written on your headstones. "Here lie Doris and Ida. They had enough." When *I* die it's going to read "Here lies Lucille. She wanted *more*." And then you and Doris can come visit me every month. You would come visit me, wouldn't you? I mean, I'd be right in the neighborhood ... just a headstone's throw away. (*Laughing.*) Get it? A *head*stone's throw.

IDA. Lucille—

LUCILLE. Will you come visit me?

IDA. Lucille.

LUCILLE. *Will you?*

IDA. Yes.

LUCILLE. (*To Doris.*) And how about you? You going to come say hello on your way over to Abe?

DORIS. Sure.

LUCILLE. And Sam. You gotta bring Sam. After all, that's where we met.

IDA. We'll bring Sam, won't we Doris?

DORIS. Sure.

(IDA tries to take the glass away from LUCILLE who pulls away.)

LUCILLE. No you won't. You're lying. You won't even tell him where I am. I'll be lying there all alone. God knows where Harry'll be.

IDA. Lucille—

LUCILLE. They should really make one big coffin for married people, don't you think? You should be able to get a king-size coffin for Christ sakes, or at least a double. You should be able to spend the rest of eternity next to your husband. Even if you don't speak, don't touch each other ... at least it's something. Instead, you got to lie there alone. All the time thinking ... saying to yourself—This is *wrong*. This is not how it should be, damn it!

IDA. Lucille, don't.

DORIS. *(Getting up.)* I'm going to bed.

LUCILLE. Why? You had enough?

DORIS. Yes.

LUCILLE. Figures.

DORIS. Let me tell you something, Lucille—

LUCILLE. Oh goodie.

DORIS. There is nothing wrong with having had enough. It just means that what you've had until now has been good and you don't have to spend the rest of your life making a fool of yourself trying to find more. *(SHE gets her small suitcase and heads for the stairs.)*

LUCILLE. *I'm* making a fool? You spend half your life at a grave, talking to a dead husband—

DORIS. (*Stopping on the landing.*) You keep Abe out of this!

IDA. (*Waving her up the stairs.*) Doris.

LUCILLE. Every month. Rain or shine. There's Doris yakking away at Abe Silverman's grave.

IDA. *Lucille.*

LUCILLE. I hope for *his* sake he was buried with cotton in his ears.

DORIS. (*Coming back into the room.*) How dare you!!

IDA. Doris, don't get excited.

DORIS. You know why I go to the cemetery every month, Lucille? Because *my* husband deserves it. Because in all the years we were married he never cheated on me once!

IDA. Come on now.

LUCILLE. So help me—

DORIS. Not *once!*

IDA. *Doris.*

DORIS. (*Approaching Lucille.*) He didn't have to cheat because our marriage was *good.* Our marriage meant something!

LUCILLE. I'm warning you.

IDA. *Lucille.*

DORIS. So don't take it out on me because your husband never loved you!!

(*LUCILLE throws her wine in Doris's face.*

DORIS puts her hand on her chest and begins breathing heavily.)

IDA. You all right?
DORIS. I just ... need ... my milk.

(IDA quickly gets the glass of milk and hands it to Doris.)

DORIS. Thank you. *(Takes the glass, raises it to her lips then throws the milk in Lucille's face.)*
IDA. Enough! Enough!

(IDA takes some napkins and cleans the carpet as DORIS and LUCILLE clean themselves off.)

IDA. Look at you. Just *look* at you! What's happened to us?!
DORIS. I'll tell you what's happened! Nothing means anything anymore! *(Indicating Lucille.)* This one here only wants to sleep around—
LUCILLE. Oh, please.
DORIS. *(To Ida.)*—And you, you only want to make a fool of yourself chasing after Sam.
IDA. Don't be ridiculous.
DORIS. *Ridiculous?* If we hadn't told him not to take you, you would've walked into Selma's wedding and made a complete fool of yourself!
IDA. *(Stunned. Confused.)* What?
LUCILLE. It certainly didn't seem to take him long to get over the loss.
DORIS. And to think I had second thoughts.

IDA. You told him ... (*SHE stops as the realization of it all sinks in.*) And you knew ...? All the time ...? You watched me get dressed. You watched me make-up ... and you knew. (*To Doris.*) When I was telling you everything I felt, everything I wanted ... you knew. (*To Lucille.*) You watched me make a fool of myself when he walked in here with Mildred ... and you *knew* ... *both* of you. (*To Doris.*) I figured you wouldn't understand but I never thought you'd try to stop it.

DORIS. We just wanted to—

IDA. What about what *I* wanted? Did you ever think for *one second,* what *I* wanted?! And who put the two of you in charge of my life?!

LUCILLE. We were only concerned with—

IDA. (*Becoming furious.*) To hell with your concern! You weren't concerned with me. You were concerned with *yourselves*. (*To Doris.*) You couldn't stand the idea that I didn't want to go to the cemetery, that maybe I wanted to do something else with my life. (*To Lucille.*) And you, you couldn't stand the fact that maybe Sam was interested in *me* and not you.

LUCILLE. I could have any man I wanted.

IDA. But not Sam!

LUCILLE. I don't want Sam!

IDA. I saw the way you flirted. "Why don't you come to the cemetery with us, Sam?" "Maybe you and *I* could get together, Sam!"

LUCILLE. I was just trying to—

IDA. You were just trying to get him into bed is what you were trying!

LUCILLE. No!

IDA. That's all you've done since Harry died!

LUCILLE. I haven't been to bed with a man since Harry died!

(*Pause. IDA and DORIS look at her.*)

LUCILLE. I wanted everyone to know I was fine. That I didn't give a damn! That ... (*Pause. Holding back her tears.*) They don't come any better than me. I don't care who he had ...! If he was up there looking down I wanted him to see me with other men or to close his eyes like *I* did. For *three years* ... I really wanted to do that. But I couldn't ... not even once. (*Sadly, quietly.*) I never said I slept with anyone. I said I go out and ... maybe I threw in a couple of extra names here and there but I never said I slept with anyone. *You* always said ... I just never denied it.

IDA. (*Pause.*) I'm going to bed. (*SHE heads for the stairs.*)

DORIS. Ida.

IDA. Take which ever rooms you want.

(*IDA goes up stairs and exits to the bedroom. There is a moment as DORIS looks to LUCILLE who has her back to her.*)

DORIS. (*Gently.*) How about one more glass of wine? A night cap.

LUCILLE. I've had enough.

(*DORIS takes her small suitcase and begins walking upstairs. SHE stops and turns to LUCILLE, who still has her back to her. SHE tries to say something but can't. SHE exits to the bedroom as LUCILLE pulls off her wig and the LIGHTS fade out.*)

Scene 3

Ida's living room. The following morning.
The room is a mess, filled with reminders of last night.
A very hung over IDA comes down the stairs wearing her robe and holding a wet rag to her forehead. SHE walks very slowly through the living room and exits to the kitchen. After a moment she re-enters with a glass of water and a bottle of aspirin. SHE sits down on the couch and proceeds to swallow several aspirin as LUCILLE, also looking the worse for wear in a matching jogging outfit, makes her way carefully down the stairs.

LUCILLE. (*Re the aspirin.*) You going to finish those?
IDA. Why?

LUCILLE. If you're not I'd like to have some. If you are I'll go into the kitchen now and cut my head off.

(IDA holds out the aspirin and the glass. LUCILLE takes them from her.)

LUCILLE. Thank you. *(SHE swallows some aspirin with the water. SHE looks to IDA who says nothing.)* Maybe I could call Sam, explain to him everything—
IDA. *(Angrily.)* I think it's a little late for that.
LUCILLE. I'm sorry. I never should have interfered. It's just that Doris and I saw you getting so involved and ... and I guess we panicked a little at the thought of our threesome breaking up.
IDA. Well, you certainly managed to stop that from happening.
LUCILLE. *(With tears in her eyes.)* Please don't hate me.
IDA. Stop it. Come on ... I'm not going to hate you. I may not like you for a while *(Getting up.)* Help me clean up. Look at what this place looks like.
LUCILLE. We'll tidy up a little, it'll look perfect.

(THEY begin cleaning up. After a moment IDA comes back to Lucille.)

IDA. (*Stopping, suddenly.*) How could you think I wouldn't understand what you were going through over Harry?

(*LUCILLE looks at her, unable to respond. IDA takes her in her arms and strokes her face. SHE then goes back to cleaning up. SHE picks up the mirror she used last night to do her make-up and looks at herself.*)

IDA. Oh my God.
LUCILLE. What?
IDA. I'm looking into the future. Right now I can see exactly what I'll look like three years after I die.

(*THEY laugh.*)

IDA. Maybe I should put on some of the green eye shadow to highlight the color in my cheeks.

(*As THEY laugh the DOORBELL rings.*)

IDA. Who could that be?
LUCILLE. Probably Selma to tell us she's getting divorced.
IDA. (*Looking out of the window.*) Oh God!
LUCILLE. Who is it?
IDA. Sam.

(*LUCILLE straightens herself up as best she can. IDA opens the door. SAM enters. HE looks anxious and nervous.*)

SAM. Hello, Ida.
IDA. Hello, Sam.
SAM. Hello, Lucille.
LUCILLE. Hi, Sam.
SAM. Where's Doris?
LUCILLE. Asleep. We stayed up late after we got back. You know women.
SAM. Could I talk to Ida alone for a minute?
LUCILLE. Oh sure. I'll uh ... I'll go make some tea. (*SHE walks to the kitchen, holding on to each piece of furniture along the way for balance. SHE exits.*)
SAM. (*Gathering up his nerve.*) I uh ... I uh ... I'm not sure what I came here to say. I just knew that I had to come over to see you. I guess ... I guess what I want to say is ... is that I don't want to stop seeing you.
IDA. (*Firmly.*) You already did.
SAM. Only because ... because I started to realize that there was the possibility that ... that maybe something was going to happen ... I mean, that something was developing between us that ... that—
IDA. I wasn't ready for.
SAM. That *I* wasn't ready for. When I think back, I was talking like such a big shot—ready to start a new chapter. Who was I kidding? I was terrified. All I needed was a door to run out of and

Lucille and Doris gave me one. We started talking about Selma's wedding and what it meant to take you and—

IDA. (*Angrily.*) So you asked Mildred.

SAM. Not because I had any real feelings for her. But because I *didn't* ... It felt safe ... It wasn't a nice thing to do to you or to her.

IDA. No.

SAM. Ida, that afternoon I spent here with you was one of the nicest afternoons I had since Merna died. And the nights we went out together felt wonderful. Each time I was with you I thought about Merna less and less. And that's what started to get to me. For the first time I wasn't comparing someone to Merna. I was enjoying you for just being you and ... and that frightened me.

IDA. (*Pause.*) I just want to know one thing. These last two weeks ... did you miss me?

SAM. Oh yes. (*Almost fearful.*) And you?

IDA. (*Nonchalantly.*) You were on my mind.

SAM. (*Pause.*) I've lost one woman in my life because there was nothing I could do to stop it. I don't want to lose you if there's still anything I can do to hold on.

(*IDA looks at him with tears in her eyes as SHE starts crying and laughing.*)

SAM. What?

IDA. I think somewhere right now Murry and Merna are having one hell of a laugh.

SAM. You think so?

IDA. Yeah.

(*LUCILLE enters with the tea and carefully sets the tray down on the table.*)

SAM. (*To Lucille.*) How about we forget the tea and go out for something to eat?

LUCILLE. (*Her mouth drops open as SHE becomes nauseous just at the thought.*) ... Food?

SAM. (*Excitedly.*) And then maybe we'll all go for some ice cream. I feel like a kid again.

IDA. Ice cream?

LUCILLE. We'd love to. We haven't eaten a thing.

IDA. Not a thing.

SAM. (*To Ida.*) So go get dressed and wake up Doris.

LUCILLE. (*To Ida.*) Yeah, go ahead. I'm sure she'll be famished.

IDA. I'm sure. (*Exits upstairs to the bedroom.*)

LUCILLE. (*Going over to Sam.*) I'm sorry, Sam. Doris and I should never have interfered.

SAM. (*Smiling, taking her hands.*) So where should we go to eat?

LUCILLE. Where ever you want.

SAM. There's a great kosher Chinese place over on Linden.

LUCILLE. Klein's?

SAM. No. You're thinking of Klein's Korean Kitchen on Union Turnpike. I'm talking Manny Peking.

LUCILLE. Oh, I know the place. Let me just put on some make-up. (*SHE takes some lipstick out of her bag and begins putting it on in front of the mirror.*) I want you to know, you're the only man, besides Harry, who's seen me without make-up ... and look what it did to him.

SAM. I think you look better.

(*IDA walks slowly down the stairs and stops. SHE stands frozen on the landing as SHE stares out across the room.*)

LUCILLE. (*Without looking up.*) She up?

(*IDA does not answer.*)

LUCILLE. (*Looking at her.*) Ida, she up?

(*No answer.*)

LUCILLE. Ida? (*Softly.*) Oh my God. (*Runs past Ida, up the stairs and exits to the bedroom.*)
IDA. (*Remains frozen with shock.*) Sam?
SAM. I'm here.

(*SAM goes to her. IDA throws her arms around him.*)

SAM. I'm here.

(*THEY hold each other as the LIGHTS fade out.*)

Scene 4

The cemetery. Abe's plot. Late afternoon.
Beside Abe's plot is a freshly covered grave.
There is no headstone, only a small marker
stuck in the earth. It is colder now than it was
in Act I. The sky is gray and most of the leaves
have fallen and turned brown.
LUCILLE enters wearing her fur coat, hat and
muff and clutches Doris's folding stool against
herself. SHE walks over to the grave, sets the
stool down and sits. SHE begins picking the
dead leaves out of the ivy as IDA enters. SHE
stands off to the side watching Lucille who is
unaware of her presence. After a moment IDA
approaches Lucille.

LUCILLE. (*Without looking at her.*) You'd
think they'd come by, clean this up.
    IDA. They wait until they've all fallen, then do
it all at once.
    LUCILLE. It's not right.
    IDA. (*Gently.*) What are you going to do?
    LUCILLE. (*Pause. Getting up.*) How was it
over at Murry's?
    IDA. All right. And Harry?
    LUCILLE. Sends his regards ... Sam over
at—
    IDA. Yeah.

LUCILLE. Merna's.

IDA. Yeah. (*Pause*.) Selma called me this morning.

LUCILLE. How's she doing?

IDA. They're very happy. I think this could be it.

LUCILLE. No kidding.

IDA. She got the pictures back from the affair. She said there's one of the three of us at the table.

LUCILLE. I didn't know they took one.

IDA. No one did. It's a picture of the two of us eating and Doris stuffing chicken wings into her purse.

(*THEY laugh. SAM enters, walks over to the grave and stands beside Ida. SHE takes his hand.*)

LUCILLE. Hello, Sam.

SAM. Hi, Lucille.

LUCILLE. How are you?

SAM. Good, and you?

LUCILLE. Not bad.

SAM. (*Pause*.) How old was Doris?

LUCILLE. She was ... I don't know.

IDA. Whatever she was, she was too young.

SAM. Who isn't? Merna was fifty-three.

LUCILLE. Must have been very difficult.

SAM. I always figured I would go first.

IDA. What's meant to be is what's—

LUCILLE. Don't you start that crap. (*To Sam.*) How many times have you heard that?

SAM. What else can you say?

LUCILLE. (*Bitterly*.) You can say that what's meant to be *stinks*, that's what you can say.

IDA. What good does it do?

(*Pause*.)

SAM. (*To Ida*.) We better get going.

LUCILLE. You're going out?

SAM. I'm going to visit my son, Richie.

IDA. I'm going with him to meet his new grandson.

LUCILLE. (*To Ida*.) You know when you're coming again?

IDA. I uh ... I don't know ... It's getting so cold.

LUCILLE. Yeah.

IDA. And not everybody has such a warm coat.

LUCILLE. At such a good price.

IDA. True. (*Pause*.) You coming?

LUCILLE. Go ahead. I'm just going to stay for another minute.

(*SAM picks up a small stone and places it on Doris's grave. IDA bends down and picks up a stone. SHE looks at Doris's grave for a long moment as SHE fights back the tears. SHE kisses the stone and places it beside the marker. SHE stands and kisses Lucille. The two WOMEN hug tightly.*)

IDA. I'll call you.
LUCILLE. (*To Sam.*) Be careful driving.
SAM. (*To Lucille.*) You take care of yourself.

(*HE kisses her on the cheek, then exits with Ida, arm in arm. LUCILLE looks after them for a long while as tears fill her eyes. SHE looks back at the grave and sits on the stool.*)

LUCILLE. They look good together, don't you think? Ten to one says they'll be married before the year's out ... That'll be some affair, huh? Gotta have good meat ... You could've made some haul on that one ... Me and Selma'll probably be bridesmaids ... There's a switch. Selma at somebody *else's* wedding. (*SHE laughs, then stops.*) They'll make a good couple. (*Pause.*) Probably won't see much of her. (*Fighting back tears.*) Look at this place. (*SHE begins picking out some leaves from the ivy. Her movements quicken and become more careless.*) A person shouldn't have to be picking leaves out of ivy. A person shouldn't have to spend the rest of their life taking care of a grave! I shouldn't have to come here very goddamn month to— (*SHE begins sobbing as SHE grabs leaves, rocks, anything and smashes them against the grave. Finally, SHE stops and stands up. Softly, sadly.*) I'm gonna miss you, Doris. (*SHE pulls herself together and regains her composure.*) But I'm telling you now ... I'm not coming here every month. I don't care how much time we've spent here, I'm not going to remember you and me in this place! I'm going to remember you dancing. I'm going to remember you arguing. I'm going to remember you pulling chicken wings out of your purse. (*SHE bends down, picks up a small stone and holds it to her heart as SHE looks at the grave. SHE then places the stone beside the marker.*) So ... I'll see you ... when I see you. (*SHE picks up the folding stool to take with her then changes her mind. SHE sets it back down beside the grave. SHE wraps her coat around herself, picks up her muff and is about to leave when SHE turns back to the grave.*) And listen ... If you see Harry, tell him ... Tell him I said goodbye. (*SHE walks slowly but steadily and exits as the LIGHTS fade out on the cemetery and Doris's grave.*)

End of Play

Costume Plot

DORIS
ACT I, (Sc. 1, 2, 3)

Costume # 1   Purple suit
Black camisole
Black pumps
Jewelry:
    Pin on suit
    Gold earrings
    Gold watch
    Gold bracelet
Black panty hose
Burgundy coat
Burgundy leather gloves
Burgundy purse

I, (4)

Costume # 2   Cream silk blouse
Rust pleated skirt
Rust shoes
Jewelry:
X Burgundy purse

II (1, 2)

Costume # 3   Slip
Pink bridesmaid shoes
Burgundy print robe
Pink panty hose

Costume # 4   Yellow bridesmaid dress
Jewelry:
    Gold and rhinestone
Black velvet coat
Large black purse

X Repeated articles of costume.

SAM

I (2, 3)
Costume # 1   Checked sport coat
          Brown pants
          Cream shirt
          Hunter green sweater vest
          Burgundy - taupe diamond -
          patterned tie
          Brown wing-tip shoes
          Rain coat
          Hat
          Brown socks

I (4)
Costume # 2   Repeat Costume # 1
          Strike tie and sport coat

II (1)
Costume #3   Dark 3-piece suit
          White shirt
          Burgundy - aqua tie
          Gold cuff links
          Gray wool top coat
          Black hat
          Black dress
          Black socks

II (3)
Costume # 4   Plaid shirt
          Corduroy pants
          Olive sweater
          Suede shoes
          Rain coat

II (4)
Costume # 5   Repeat #4
          Repeat wool top coat
          Repeat black hat

IDA
I (1, 2, 3)
Costume # 1   Rose - navy print two-piece -
                               dress
                               Tan - lacy shoes
                               Apron
                               Beige - black herringbone coat
                               Black - rose print scarf
                               Tan leather gloves
                               Tan clutch purse
                               Jewelry:
                                   Pin on coat
                                   Gold earrings
                                   Pearl necklace
                                   Gold watch
                                   Almond panty hose
                                   Glasses
II (1, 2)
Costume #2   Slip
                               Peach print robe
                               Brocade slippers
                               Beige panty hose over- dressed -
                               w/ pink panty hose
                               Pale blue head scarf
Costume #3   Yellow bridesmaid dress
                               Bridesmaid shoes (pink)
                               Jewelry:
                                   Crystal earrings
                                   Crystal necklace
                                   Ring
                                   Black/fur cape
                                   Black satin purse

II (3)
Costume # 4   Flowered robe
                               X Brocade slippers

II (4)
Costume #5   Purple - navy dress
                               Navy shoes
                               Purple coat
                               Purple print scarf
                               Navy gloves
                               Navy leather purse
                               Pearl earrings

LUCILLE
I (1, 2, 3)
Costume # 1   Fuchsia pants and jacket
                               Fuchsia - orange print blouse
                               Fuchsia - orange flats
                               Jewelry:
                                   Large gold bracelet
                                   Heavy gold necklace
                               Fur coat
                               Sun glasses
                               Beige/taupe large purse
                               Suntan panty hose

I (4)
Costume #2   Black blouse
                               Black/purple print pants
                               Beaded flats
                               Purple/blue scarf
                               Beige leather gloves
                               Jewelry:
                               X Gold bracelet
                               Fur hat
                               X Fur coat
                               X Sun glasses
                               X Beige purse

II (1, 2)
Costume # 3/#5   Purple - green- black velour top
                       Purple pants
                       Beaded high top sneakers
                       Jewelry:
                           Black multi-colored stone -
                       earrings
                           X Gold bracelet
                       X Fur coat
                       X Fur hat

Costume # 4   Yellow bridesmaid dress
                       Silver bridesmaid shoes
                       Jewelry
                           Pearl/rhinestone earrings,
                           Gold rings, diamond ring
                           Sm. rhinestone brooch
                           Rhinestone ankle bracelet
                       Fur muff
                       X Fur coat
                       X Fur hat

II (3)
Costume # 5   Repeat Costume # 3
II (4)
Costume # 6   X Costume # 5 plus:
                       Fur coat
                       Fur hat
                       Muff from sofa
                       Black/gold flats
                       Black/purple/green scarf

MILDRED
Only Costume   Orange print dress
                                Purse
                                Orange gloves
                                Fur jacket
                                Orange shoes
                                Jewelry:
                                    Purple/rhinestone earrings
                                    Watch
                                    Bracelet
                                    Rhinestone ring

PROPERTY PLOT

Costume Props
ACT I, Scene 1
Telephone chair back - Ida's scarf
Telephone desk - Ida's purse with gloves, eye glass case, pocket Kleenex, dark cloth, contact lens case, contact solution, comb.

In Closet - Ida's coat
Off L.: LUCILLE - fur coat (dressing room)
                    Shoulder bag with car keys
                    cigarette case w/ cigs
                    sun glasses
                    lipstick
       DORIS - Coat (may wear from dressing rm)
                    gloves
                    scarf
                    purse with boy pix
                      scissors
                      pocket Kleenex (discard old one)
                      empty plastic bag

ACT I, Scene 4: Cemetery
Off L: LUCILLE's fur hat
       Shoulder bag from previous scene

ACT I II, Scene 1:
Onstage
    R Chair - Doris' bridesmaid dress inside out
     On piano US closed key cover - Doris' purse fully
loaded
    Off R Stairs - Ida's bridesmaid dress in garment bag
                    Ida's shoes
                    Ida's evening bag
    Off L - LUCILLE's muff

During ACT II, Scene 1

In UR quick change area LUCILLE changes into her bridesmaid dress, shoes, blond wig.

End of ACT II, Scene 2, LUCILLE needs a quick exit - has eyelashes in one hand and blond wig in other.

Into II-4 quickie for LUCILLE - fur coat from closet during II-3, fur hat; Sam gets fur muff from sofa, hands to Lucille w/stool.

ACT I, Scene 1: Blinds open, nothing on Hi-Fi, ever.

On UR desk: phone, pad & pencil, waste basket (emptied), Ida's tan clutch purse w/ eye glass case, no glasses, handkerchief, dark cloth, contact lens case, contact solution, comb, checkbook

On Desk chair L arm - lap blanket

On Chair bank - Ida's scarf

In Closet - Ida's coat (houndstooth - tan gloves, house keys)

UL shelf by door: empty dish

Off Front Door - Ida's lipstick

On Sofa: Open newspaper, left end

On R Sofa arm: child's dress/w needle & thread

On Sofa end table: unopened candy bag, crossword dictionary, instructions with threads on top

On Top of Coffee Table: crossword puzzle, with pencil (center); open News (SL), Magazines (SR); on bottom shelf (Mag toward audience)

Between R sofa arm & end table (knitting bag (scissor DS pocket)

R Chair on ACT I marks & Coffee Table on marks Sideboard:

Top Shelf - DS side - saucers & bowl for peanuts
2nd Shelf DS side - 2 cups - US side 4 wine glasses
Left drawer - napkins - right drawer - silverware
Bottom Left - Tea mat folded

Bottom Right - Sewing basket w/ lime spool; beige spool to prop table

On Sideboard - 3 saucers w/2 cups on top - 1 cup & candy dish

On Chair end table - Pipe rack

On Piano: Pictures (US), Ashtray (DS) keyboard covered

ACT I, Scene 1

Off Right in Tomb shelf: Oven mitt; tray w/tea pot w/ tea, sugar bowl w/packets of sugar & Equal, 3 napkins, 3 teaspoons; - Plate of cookies (I-1); Tin of cocktail unsalted nuts (I-1)

I-3 Props: remove dirty cups, etc. Reload tray w/3 tea cups, saucers, napkins, teaspoons, sugar, creamer w/skim milk & plate of cookies; - Small tray w/teapot w/tea & crochet as hot pad; plastic ziplock bag with lots of cookies inside (I-3); Ida's eyeglasses - personal.

Off Left: (Door)

Lucille - Fur coat, Shoulder bag containing: car keys, cigarette case & lighter, matches, sun glasses, sm. mirror, lipstick

Doris - canvas stool; purse w/pix of boy, scissors, pocket Kleenex (discard old) plastic bag (empty out leaves); Coat, Scarf, Gloves

Act I, Scene 2: Cemetery

3 stones at Abe's (SL) & one at Murry's (SR); replace Abe's leaves (should have been done from previous show); token leaves on L bench - leave on L marker; Doris canvas stool (she should have it from exit of Sc. 1)

ACT I, Scene 3 On Stage No Change

Off L Door: Brown bag of chicken livers -Sam; Car keys - Sam- personal; coat & hat - Sam

ACT I, Scene 4: Cemetery:
Leaves replaced (recycled from dresser during I-3)

Reset stone from headstone
Remove leaves from left bench
replace Ida's stone

Off Left:

Doris - Canvas stool (same as I-2); rides out with her; purse w/scissors, Kleenex, (discard old), plastic bag (empty out leaves),

Lucille - Fur hat (added), fur coat, shoulder bag, Net bag containing grapes on top, instant Sanka, cream cheese, oranges, bagels, etc.; Greek cup of Diet Coke w/Equal w/lid

Top of Act II, Scene 1 - Blinds open, nothing on Hi-Fi

Strike: pipe rack from chair end table, ashtray stays but clean; tea mat from coffee table (replace to bottom DS sideboard); small child dress to knit bag

Re-set: Sideboard All cups and saucers except 3

At Sideboard: Step stool (sewing basket on top w/lime spool); trivet for iron - US end of sideboard; Minora (no candles); & box of candles (center); Ironing board with iron plugged in

Change newspapers & magazines (time lapse) - coffee table bottom shelf

Coffee table should be clear

Right Chair - Doris' dress inside out

Phone table - Ida's black purse with eye glass case, dark cloth, contact lens case & liquid, & Kleenex & checkbook

House keys strike from dish at door to Ida's evening bag on offstage stairs

Place in dish at door - Lucille's lipstick

In Closet - Ida's coat & Doris' coat

Piano - (key cover closed) - Doris' purse on US end with bottom:

1) squished with open napkin
2) kiwi
3) grapes

4) apple
5) 2 oranges
6) banana
7) chicken wings
8) cookies
On top 9) 3 pieces of wedding cake, all wrapped in wedding napkins

Piano bench - opened suitcase; jewelry soft wrapper case; cosmetic bag w/ compact & puff, lipstick, eye shadow, blush brush, sm. hair brush (all above in bag)
  Atomizer perfume
  Hand mirror
  Nightgown
  Off Right Stage:
  Top of stairs - Ida's dress in garment bag, unzipped
                    Ida's shoes
                    Ida's evening purse w/ pocket
                    Kleenex, house keys, mascara &
                    hand mirror;
                    Make-up mirror
                    Large spool of beige thread (lime
                    spool back to sewing basket)
UR quick change for ACT II - Lucille - dress, shoes, blond wig
  Off Right Stage (kitchen):
  Lucille's lipstick w. mirror end (II-1)
  Wet compress II-3 (gets placed on railing top during Ida quick change)
  glass of milk (II-2)
  Lucille's sneakers (II-3)
  Bottle of aspirin w/ top off (II-3)
  Glass of water (II-3)
  Tray w/ 3 cups & saucers (II-3)
                    Teapot (empty)

Creamer
Sugar bowl
3 spoons
3 napkins
Off Down Right - Canvas Stool
Off Left (II-1) Lucille - suitcase
 fur muff
 fur coat & fur hat
 garment bag
 Make-up case w/ mirror in lid
  false eyelashes
  Johnson duo liquid adhesive
  blue & green eye shadow
  mascara
  lipstick
  comb
  blush brush
  black pencil liner
Mildred - Purse & gloves (II-1) personal
Sam - Coat & hat & car keys (II-1) personal
Flower arrangement "Bonfigliano" (II-2)
Bottle of white wine w/wine (II-2)
Lucille's cigarette case (loaded with cigarettes) (II-2)
ACT II, Scene 2 - No stage change
ACT II, Scene 3 - No stage change
Off Left Cemetery ACT II, Scene 4:
Fresh grave set w/3 stones stage right of grave (set intermission)
Ida's stone should be struck off top of Murry's to grass

PERISHABLES
True Blue regular cigarettes
Butane
Decaf tea
Skim milk

Oatmeal cookies
fake aspirin
Equal
Peanuts, unsalted, cocktail
pocket Kleenex
Candy (spiced sm. gum drops)
table napkins
cocktail napkins
ziplock plastic bags
sandwich bags for leaves
green grapes (or false grapes)
Greek coffee containers w/lids
hard contact lens liquid
wedding cake
white grape juice
perfume atomizer
Ivy
make-up
dish liquid soap
leaves
powdered non-fat milk

RUNNING PROPS

During I-2 (cemetery) if there is one teapot and one tray: then reload tray w/ 3 cups, saucers, spoons, napkins, creamer w/skim milk, sugar with sugar & Equal packets, plate of cookies; Sm. tray with teapot with more tea & doily as pot holder

I-3 - No stage change

During I-3 re-ivy Abe's grave & stone, leaves off bench, & replace Ida's stone

End of ACT I - Right Props: standby to receive Lucille's net shopping bag, coffee cup & Doris' grave stool; place canvas stool DR for end of ACT II

Intermission - Set up II-1; Set up II-4: fresh grave, stones, re-ivy

During II-1 (about 8 mins. in) Right Props: stand by to take step stool and ironing board & iron from the ladies when they exit off R - kitchen; Left Props: stand by to close venetian shade

II-2 No stage change

II-3 No stage change - Left Props: stand by to open venetian shade

Into II-4 (cemetery) Prop Man: get muff from sofa & hand to Lucille & canvas stool

Canvas stool down right

Other Publications for Your Interest

I'M NOT RAPPAPORT
(LITTLE THEATRE—COMEDY)
By HERB GARDNER

5 men, 2 women—Exterior

Just when we thought there would never be another joyous, laugh-filled evening on Broadway, along came this delightful play to restore our faith in the Great White Way. If you thought *A Thousand Clowns* was wonderful, wait til you take a look at *I'm Not Rappaport!* Set in a secluded spot in New York's Central Park, the play is about two octogenarians determined to fight off all attempts to put them out to pasture. Talk about an odd couple! Nat is a lifelong radical determined to fight injustice (real or imagined) who is also something of a spinner of fantasies. He has a delightful repertoire of eccentric personas, which makes the role an actor's dream. The other half of this unlikely partnership is Midge, a Black apartment super who spends his days in the park hiding out from tenants, who want him to retire. "Rambunctiously funny."—N.Y. Post. "A warm and entertaining evening."—W.W. Daily. **Tony Award Winner, Best Play 1986. Posters.**

(#11071)

CROSSING DELANCEY
(LITTLE THEATRE—COMEDY)
By SUSAN SANDLER

2 men, 3 women—Comb. Interior/Exterior.

Isabel is a young Jewish woman who lives alone and works in a NYC bookshop. When she is not pining after a handsome author who is one of her best customers, she is visiting her grandmother—who lives by herself in the "old neighborhood", Manhattan's Lower East Side. Isabel is in no hurry to get married, which worries her grandmother. The delightfully nosey old lady hires an old friend who is—can you believe this in the 1980's?—a matchmaker. Bubbie and the matchmaker come up with a Good Catch for their Isabel—Sam, a young pickle vendor. Same is no *schlemiel*, though. He likes Isabel; but he knows he is going to have to woo her, which he proceeds to do. When Isabel realizes what a cad the author is, and what a really nice man Sam is, she begins to respond; and the end of the play is really a beginning, ripe with possibilities for Isabel and "An amusing interlude for theatregoers who may have thought that simple romance and sentimentality had long since been relegated to television sitcoms...tells its unpretentious story believeably, rarely trying to make its gag lines, of which there are many, upstage its narration or out-shine its heart."—N.Y. Times. "A warm and loving drama...a welcome addition to the growing body of Jewish dramatic work in this country."—Jewish Post and Opinion.

(#5739)